RY

S0-AVH-380

Sacramento, CA 95814

05/13

CLUB
CSI:™

The Case of the Plagued Play

by David Lewman

Simon Spotlight

New York   London   Toronto   Sydney   New Delhi

SIMON SPOTLIGHT

An imprint of Simon & Schuster Children's Publishing Division
1230 Avenue of the Americas, New York, New York 10020
© 2013 by CBS Broadcasting Inc. and Entertainment AB Funding LLC.
All Rights Reserved. CSI: CRIME SCENE INVESTIGATION in USA is a trademark of CBS Broadcasting Inc. and outside USA is a trademark of Entertainment AB Funding LLC.
All rights reserved, including the right of reproduction in whole or in part in any form.
SIMON SPOTLIGHT and colophon are registered trademarks of Simon & Schuster, Inc.
For information about special discounts for bulk purchases, please contact Simon & Schuster Special Sales at 1-866-506-1949 or business@simonandschuster.com.
Manufactured in the United States of America 0413 FFG
First Edition 10 9 8 7 6 5 4 3 2 1
ISBN 978-1-4424-7260-0 (pbk)
ISBN 978-1-4424-7261-7 (hc)
ISBN 978-1-4424-7262-4 (eBook)
Library of Congress Control Number 2013931104

Chapter 1

Mrs. Gordon walked between the desks of her students, passing back their graded assignments. When she got to Theo's desk, she paused.

She'd been teaching eighth-grade English at Woodlands Junior High School for sixteen years, and Theo's assignment was one of the finest pieces of student writing she'd ever seen. It had been a pleasure to read.

"Great job, Theo," she said, handing him the thick bundle of stapled pages. "You must have worked really hard on this."

"Thanks," Theo murmured. He looked at the grade Mrs. Gordon had written on the front page: A+!

Theo sat staring at the paper, looking slightly stunned.

Mark, the student sitting next to Theo, sneaked a glance at Theo's grade. When he saw the A+, he frowned. Mark had been really proud of the A he'd gotten—until he saw Theo's A+. Now he just felt envious.

He was about to feel even more envious.

After she'd returned the last graded paper, Mrs. Gordon made her way back to her desk at the front of the class. "I was really pleased with how each of you handled this long-term assignment," she said. "It's not easy writing a full-length play, but you did quite well. Very impressive."

The students smiled, proud of themselves. Mrs. Gordon was notorious for being a tough grader, so it was unusual for her to talk so positively about their homework.

"In fact," she continued, "you've done so well that Miss Farrell and I have a surprise for you." Miss Farrell was the other eighth-grade English teacher at their Nevada junior high school. She'd assigned her class to write plays too.

Mrs. Gordon smiled. "One of your plays is going

to receive a full-scale production right here at Woodlands Junior High. It'll be this year's school play!"

The students looked excited. They'd never heard of a play written by a student being chosen as the school play.

Each student secretly wondered and hoped, *Did they pick* my *play?*

A girl named Chelsea raised her hand. "Yes, Chelsea?" Mrs. Gordon asked, calling on her.

"Have you and Miss Farrell already picked which play is going to be put on?" Chelsea asked, bouncing her knee and tapping her desk with a pencil.

Mrs. Gordon nodded. "Yes, we have," she said. "We were in complete agreement."

She paused, keeping her students in suspense. She wished the whole class would pay such close attention every day.

"Whose is it?" Chelsea asked, unable to bear the tension any longer.

"Theo's," Mrs. Gordon announced. "Woodlands Junior High will be putting on Theo's play, *Nobody's Home.*"

Every student's head turned toward Theo. He

looked down at his script, embarrassed by all the attention.

"Way to go, Theo!" said a friendly kid named Sam. "Awesome!" He started applauding, and the others joined in. Except for Mark.

Mrs. Gordon held up her hands to stop their applause and regain their attention. "I'll be directing the play myself," she said. "Auditions will be next week, and I encourage all of you to try out. You don't need to have acted before. I think Theo's play is going to be a lot of fun!"

The kids in the class whispered and chattered. Everyone was excited by Mrs. Gordon's surprising announcement.

Except for Theo and Mark. They didn't look excited at all.

Chapter 2

On a Monday a month later, Hannah, Ben, and Corey were eating lunch at their usual table in the school cafeteria. The three seventh graders had been friends since kindergarten, and they hung out together all the time—in classes, at lunch, and when they met as the only members of Club CSI.

They enjoyed their forensic science class with Miss Hodges so much that a while back they'd decided to form a club dedicated to solving crimes by collecting and analyzing hard evidence. So far their club had already solved five mysteries!

At that moment, Corey was staring at the food on his tray.

"Something wrong with your lunch?" Ben asked.

"There must be," Hannah teased. "Usually it'd be gone by now."

Corey shook his head, keeping his eyes on his food. "There's nothing wrong with it. I'm just practicing mindfulness."

Hannah looked puzzled. "*What*-fulness?"

"Mindfulness," Corey repeated.

"Does it involve trying to hypnotize a piece of chicken?" Ben wondered.

Corey finally looked up from the tray of food. "Our coach is teaching us mindfulness."

"Which coach?" Hannah asked. Corey played on a lot of teams.

"Basketball," Corey answered.

"And what is mindfulness, exactly?" Ben asked. "When you're full of mind?"

Corey nodded. "Sort of. I think it's when you're in the zone, concentrating on what you're doing, not distracted by anything. Coach says it's what makes the difference between a good player and a great player." He grinned. "That, and running laps."

Hannah was intrigued. That kind of concentration could help her in ballet class. Lately she'd had trouble focusing while she was dancing. She

kept getting distracted by Club CSI's cases.

Though at the moment there was no case.

"How do you practice mindfulness?" she asked.

Corey gestured toward his lunch tray. "You do these different mindfulness exercises. Coach said instead of just inhaling your lunch, which, by the way, I don't do. . . ."

"If you tried to inhale your lunch, you'd choke," Ben agreed.

"Right," Hannah said. "It just *seems* as though you inhale your lunch."

"Yeah, I guess," Corey said, not sure if that was an insult. "Anyway, Coach says you should try being mindful of your lunch. Before you eat it, look at it."

All three looked at their lunches intently.

"What colors do you see? What shapes? What patterns?" Corey asked.

Ben and Hannah looked down at their trays even more intently. They'd each gone with the turkey sandwich today, while Corey had chosen the grilled chicken and veggies.

"I see a sandwich shape," Ben said.

"Now smell your lunch," Corey prompted, taking a big sniff.

"Smells good," Hannah said. "I think we should eat it. Lunch period doesn't last forever."

"Should we listen to our lunches, too?" Ben asked. He leaned down and put his right ear close to his sandwich. "Hello? Anything to say?"

"*Yummy, yummy!*" Hannah whispered intensely. "*Time to eat!*"

Corey speared a piece of grilled chicken with his fork. He held it up. "Okay, now go ahead and take a bite, but don't swallow it. Feel it in your mouth and really taste it."

All three kids took big bites and then rolled the food around in their mouths, tasting it. Hannah and Ben made funny faces, but they really did taste their bites of food. They noticed each part of their sandwiches—the bread, the lettuce, the turkey, the mustard . . .

Finally, they chewed and swallowed.

"You know," Ben admitted, "your coach may be on to something here. I noticed the taste of that bite a lot more than the bites I took before it."

Corey smiled and nodded. "He says you can practice mindfulness while you're doing almost anything—showering, washing your hands in the sink, and even playing fetch with your dog . . ."

Hannah picked up her carton of milk. "I'm not sure Molly would put up with me staring at a ball for a long time before I threw it. She'd start barking like crazy."

"Dogs are good at concentrating, though," Ben said. "I've seen Molly stare at a squirrel like there were laser beams coming out of her eyes."

"Luckily, she just stares," Hannah said. "I think she'd really like to chase squirrels, but I don't let her. And I don't think she'd know what to do with a squirrel if she got one."

Crash! A boy on the far side of the cafeteria accidentally dropped his tray of food. Lots of kids whooped, laughed, and cheered.

"Even a dog couldn't concentrate in this cafeteria," Hannah noted. "It's so loud and crazy."

Corey picked up a shiny red apple and then looked at it. "That's why this is such a good place to practice mindfulness. If you can block out all the noises and movements and chaos here, you'll be better at doing it on the basketball court."

Ben looked around. He'd never really noticed how much was going on in the cafeteria before: all the sounds—knives and forks clinking, kids laughing, trays clattering onto the metal rack by the trash cans; all the smells—hot casseroles, warm bread, chocolate milk; and the sights—kids eating at tables, Mrs. Collins serving food behind the counter, posters all over the walls . . .

"What's with all the posters?" Ben asked, noticing them for the first time. "What are they for?"

Hannah twisted around in her chair to look at the posters Ben was talking about. "Oh," she said. "Those are for the school play, *Nobody's Home*."

"I heard about that. I didn't know the name of the play," said Ben.

"I'm glad you brought it up, though," Hannah continued. "My friend Kelly's in it. She's in my ballet class, but she's actually had to miss a lot of classes this month because of all the play rehearsals."

"Sounds intense," said Ben.

"It is," Hannah replied. "The cast has been working really hard, and they want lots of people to come see it. I promised her I'd go. I was hoping you guys would come with me on opening night."

"When's that?" Corey asked, chewing his apple.

"This Friday," Hannah said casually. She was

expecting resistance to her suggestion. She knew Friday night was when Ben watched one of his favorite shows on the sci-fi channel. And Corey almost always went to some sporting event on Friday nights—either one he was playing in or one he wanted to see.

But she was pleasantly surprised.

"Sounds good," Ben said.

"I'm in," Corey added.

"Well, that was easy!" Hannah exclaimed. "So you really want to go see the play?"

Ben nodded. "Absolutely. I heard it was written by an eighth grader right here at our very own Woodlands Junior High. Impressive."

"That's right," Hannah confirmed. "Kelly says this kid named Theo wrote it for his English class, and he had no idea it would end up being performed as the school play."

"*Nobody's Home,*" Corey mused. "What's it about?" He quickly polished off a granola bar. Apparently, he was done with mindfulness for the moment. "Sports?" he asked hopefully, still chewing. "'Home' could be home plate."

"It's a mystery," Ben said.

"You mean no one knows what it's about?" Corey said, puzzled.

"No, I mean the play is a mystery," Ben repeated.

"So you don't know," Corey said.

"Yes, I do!" Ben said, frustrated. "It's a mystery!"

Hannah came to their aid. "What Ben means is that the play itself tells a mystery story, like a who-dunit."

"Ohhhh," Corey said, getting it. "Okay. What's the *mystery* about? Sports?"

"Kelly told me it's about five siblings who inherit this mansion after their aunt dies," Hannah explained. "One of the siblings doesn't want to share the big house with the others, so he or she tries to scare them away by making it seem like the mansion is haunted."

"Which is it?" Corey asked.

Hannah was confused. "Which is what?"

"Which is it?" Corey repeated. "He or she?"

"Oh," Hannah said, understanding. "I don't know. Everyone working on the play is keeping the ending a secret, so it'll be a surprise."

"I'll bet it's one of the sisters," Corey said. "The brothers wouldn't mind sharing the mansion. They could hang out together and play games."

"It's not fair to make that assumption about all girls," Hannah protested.

Before an argument could break out, Ben pointed to a dark-haired girl across the cafeteria. "Isn't that your friend Kelly?" he asked. "The one who's in the play?"

Hannah looked to where Ben was pointing. "Yes!" she said. "That's Kelly."

"Isn't she in eighth grade?" Corey asked.

"Yeah, but we're in the same ballet class," Hannah explained. She waved until Kelly noticed. Then Hannah motioned for her to come over to their table. Kelly nodded and started over.

"The members of the cast are selling tickets every day this week at lunch," Hannah said. "We can buy three for opening night before the show sells out."

"Is it really going to sell out?" Corey asked, surprised. "Is the school play usually that popular?"

Hannah nodded. "This one is. I've heard lots of people talking about it. I think everyone's curious about a play written by someone here at Woodlands. Maybe it'll have characters based on kids we know. Or teachers. That could be really funny."

Kelly arrived at their table. "Hi, Hannah," she said with a little wave.

"Hi, Kelly," Hannah said, smiling. "We want to buy three tickets for opening night. These are my friends Ben and Corey."

Kelly pulled an envelope out of her bag. "Opening night? Maybe you should pick another night."

"Why?" Hannah asked. "We're dying to see it."

Kelly sighed. "Okay, but I just hope we're ready. Things haven't exactly been going smoothly."

"Maybe everyone is just nervous," said Corey, trying to help. "I almost always get jitters before a big game."

Kelly gave a little smile. "Maybe," she said. "But I've been dancing for years, and I'm used to being onstage. Lots of the other cast members are into sports or singing or dancing, too, so we're used to stage fright."

As Hannah paid for her ticket, she watched Kelly closely. It wasn't like her to sound so negative. Kelly looked seriously worried about something.

Corey and Ben dug out money from their wallets.

Kelly realized something as she handed tickets to Ben and Corey. "Wait a minute," she said. "You're

14.

the guys who solved those mysteries with Hannah, aren't you?"

Corey felt proud, but tried to look modest. "Yep," he said. "We're Club CSI. At your service."

Kelly bit her lip, thinking. "Actually," she said slowly, "I might be able to use your service. I think I might have a case for you."

Ben, Corey, and Hannah looked interested. It had been a while since they'd had a case to work on, and they were eager to investigate a new mystery.

"Sure!" Hannah said enthusiastically. "What's the case?"

The bell rang, signaling the end of lunch period.

"I've gotta run," Kelly said, looking around. "My next class is way on the other side of the building, and my teacher says if I'm late again, I'll get detention. Which would be really terrible during our last week of rehearsals."

"That's okay," Hannah said. "Why don't we meet you after school?"

"I've got rehearsal," Kelly said. "But could you meet me in front of the auditorium right before?"

"We'll be there," Corey said, grinning. "Full of mindfulness."

Chapter 3

After school, Corey, Hannah, and Ben met in the hallway right outside the big double doors leading into the auditorium. As they waited for Kelly, they saw other members of the cast go inside for rehearsal. A couple of them glanced at the three seventh graders, wondering why they were hanging around. The others were too busy staring at their scripts, making sure they remembered their lines. Corey even saw the playwright, Theo, walking into the auditorium. Theo was on the junior varsity basketball team, and Corey was on the varsity team, so they knew each other, but not well.

Finally, Kelly ran down the hallway toward them. "Sorry I'm late," she said, breathing hard.

"That's okay," Hannah said. "So what's this case?"

Mrs. Gordon opened one of the auditorium doors and looked out into the hallway. "Kelly?" she called. "Let's go. We're ready to start rehearsing."

Kelly looked at the members of Club CSI and then looked back at Mrs. Gordon. "Would it be all right if my three friends watched rehearsal?" she asked.

Ben and Corey looked at Hannah. Was Kelly really expecting them to sit through a whole rehearsal? Hannah wanted to help her friend, so she gave them a look that said *Come on, please?* Corey sighed, but Ben gave a little nod, and Corey shrugged.

Mrs. Gordon hesitated. "Well, I'd planned on keeping these final rehearsals before opening night strictly closed. I don't want the play's surprise ending to be spoiled. The only person not in the play who will be watching today is Theo, and since he wrote the play, he already knows what's going to happen."

"You can trust my friends, Mrs. Gordon. This is Club CSI. Besides, we're only working on the first act today, right?" Kelly asked, not ready to give up yet.

Mrs. Gordon nodded. "That's true." She smiled at Ben, Corey, and Hannah. "It's nice to meet you, Club CSI. I've heard a lot about you from your club's advisor, Miss Hodges. You three are really good at solving mysteries, but don't try to solve the mystery in the play until you see it on opening night." Mrs. Gordon winked at them and then turned back to Kelly. "All right, your friends may come in. But I'm going to ask your three guests to sit at the back of the auditorium and to keep as quiet as possible. Remember, even though it's called a play . . ."

"We're working," Kelly finished. Mrs. Gordon had drilled this motto into the actors' brains at every rehearsal.

"Right!" Mrs. Gordon said. "Now, let's go!"

They filed into the auditorium. Onstage, the set for the first act was in place. It was a pretty convincing replica of a room in a mansion, with big paintings on the walls, heavy drapes on the tall windows, and a large fireplace.

"Cool," Corey said. "I wouldn't mind living in a huge house like that."

"So many more places to lose stuff," Hannah pointed out.

"No problem," Corey said. "If I lost anything, I'd just have my servants find it."

The three friends sat in the last row of the

theater. Theo sat by himself in one of the middle rows. Mrs. Gordon said they could all help her by letting her know if any of the cast members were hard to hear or understand.

She turned to the five actors standing onstage. "Remember to send your voices right to the back of the hall. What's it called when you do that?"

"Projecting!" the five kids answered loudly.

"I had no problem hearing that," Ben whispered to Hannah and Corey.

"All right," Mrs. Gordon said, taking a seat in the third row and opening a notebook. "I think the opening's in pretty good shape, so let's start with the third scene. Places, please."

The scene went fairly smoothly. It started with one of the brothers and one of the sisters who had inherited the mansion arguing onstage. Soon another brother and another sister joined them. All four seemed to know their lines and where they were supposed to move (which Mrs. Gordon called their "blocking").

Club CSI watched the scene, getting caught up in the story of *Nobody's Home*. "They're good," Corey whispered to Hannah, who nodded.

"It looks like fun to be in a play," she whispered back. "Maybe I'll try out next year."

But suddenly the scene came to a halt. Four actors stood onstage, waiting. Nothing happened.

"Kelly!" Mrs. Gordon called from her seat in the auditorium. "Where are you?"

Kelly peeked out from the side of the stage. "Sorry, Mrs. Gordon, but I'm supposed to enter carrying a wet umbrella, and it's not here with the props."

Mrs. Gordon sighed and called out the stage manager's name. "Courtney?"

Courtney appeared next to Kelly.

"Where's the umbrella?"

Courtney shrugged. "We can't find it. It's not in its bucket underneath the prop table. I've looked everywhere."

"All right," Mrs. Gordon said, writing a note. "Let's start from right before Kelly's entrance. Kelly, just pretend you have the umbrella. And let's try to keep going. Don't stop unless you have to."

They started again. Kelly entered, pretending to shake off the water from an umbrella. It was supposed to be raining outside. She was playing

an accident-prone sister named Penelope who was always late.

"Seems like Kelly's taking the part to heart, losing her umbrella," Ben whispered to Corey, who stifled a laugh.

But soon it was all right to laugh, because Penelope had several clumsy moments that were really funny. She knocked over a gong, then turned and walked right into a potted plant.

"For a ballet dancer, she's really good at being clumsy," Corey joked quietly.

"Maybe she's good at acting clumsy *because* she's a ballet dancer," Hannah replied. "She's got great control of her body."

The four other actors seemed inspired by Kelly's comic performance. And the laughter from Club CSI. The scene went well.

For a while.

Then an eighth grader named Tim stopped in front of a bookshelf and just stood there saying, "Um . . ."

Everyone stared at him.

Then he asked, "Line?"

Courtney started to read his next line to him

from offstage, but Mrs. Gordon interrupted.

"Tim, we're past the point where you can call for your line if you forget it," she said. "When we open this Friday, you won't be able to call for lines. You'll just have to keep going."

Tim looked out into the auditorium. "But I didn't forget my line, Mrs. Gordon."

"Then why didn't you say it?" Mrs. Gordon asked, confused.

"Because I never learned it," he explained. "It's a long speech, and I'm supposed to be holding open an old book, so you said it would be okay if I taped the speech inside the book and read it."

"Okay," Mrs. Gordon said slowly. "Then why didn't you *read* your line?"

Tim gestured toward the bookshelf. "Because the old book isn't on the old bookshelf." The other cast members giggled.

Courtney started to come onto the stage to look for the missing book, but Mrs. Gordon stopped her. "Courtney, please stay offstage. Read Tim's speech from your script, and let's keep going."

"Sorry," Courtney said as she scurried offstage. She read Tim's speech somewhat woodenly while

Tim moved his lips, pretending to read from an invisible book.

The rest of rehearsal went okay, but the actors seemed to be losing their excitement. So many stops had ruined the atmosphere. When they were almost out of time, Mrs. Gordon called the five cast members to the edge of the stage. They sat there with their feet dangling over the side.

Mrs. Gordon gave them lots of notes she'd written down during rehearsal—when to be louder, when to be softer, when to be more energetic, when to turn their faces out toward the audience so everyone could see their expressions. It seemed as though there were an awful lot of ways for an actor to mess up.

All the cast members wrote down Mrs. Gordon's notes, scribbling like mad on the backs of their scripts.

"Finally," she said, "please remember to *keep going*. Even if something goes wrong. I don't care if the roof caves in, keep going until the fire department arrives. *Then* you can stop."

The cast members laughed. A little nervously. They all knew rehearsal hadn't gone smoothly, and in just a few days they'd have to perform *Nobody's Home* for a real, live audience full of their friends and families.

"All right," Mrs. Gordon said, standing up. "I'm going to find the missing props and make sure everything's all in place for tomorrow's rehearsal. See you then. Same time, same theater."

She walked up the steps and onto the stage and then went back to the prop table. Theo had left while Mrs. Gordon was giving notes, and the cast members and the stage manager looked eager to get home, eat dinner, and start their homework, but Kelly stopped them at the back of the auditorium.

"Guys? Can you stay a couple more minutes?" she asked.

"Sure," Tim said. "What for?"

Kelly gestured toward Hannah, Corey, and Ben. "I've asked Club CSI to investigate what's been going on with our show." She sat down next to Hannah. "As you could see during rehearsal, we've been having a lot of problems with props and things going missing."

"How long has this been going on?" Hannah asked.

"About a week," Kelly said.

Another girl, Melissa, spoke up. "Mrs. Gordon thinks it's just a bunch of accidents, but some of us think it's something else."

"Like what?" Corey asked.

Melissa looked around nervously. "Like someone is trying to sabotage the play."

The other kids nodded seriously.

"Who?" Ben asked. "Who would do that?"

They all looked stumped. Then a girl named Tessa, the youngest member of the cast, timidly raised her hand. "I heard the auditorium is haunted," she said, her eyes growing wide. "Maybe the ghost is stealing the props."

A boy named John snorted. "Come on! I think maybe you're getting a little too caught up in the play. Like we really *are* in a haunted mansion!"

"Whoever's doing it," Tim said, "it's really messing up our rehearsal process. We're afraid the play's going to be a disaster. Which would be totally humiliating."

Ben, Corey, and Hannah exchanged quick nods. "Don't worry," Ben said. "We'll take the case. We'll find out who is trying to sabotage the school play!"

Chapter 4

The next morning, Ben, Corey, and Hannah talked about their new case as they hurried toward their forensic science class.

"Thanks again for agreeing to take on the case, guys," Hannah said. "I really want to help Kelly out if we can."

"No problem," Ben said. "Besides, I know someone in the play too."

"You do?" Hannah said, surprised.

"Yeah," Ben said. "Well, not exactly *in* the play, but working on it. The stage manager, Courtney, is in my honors math class."

"Is she a seventh grader?" Corey asked.

They turned left into the hallway with all the

science classrooms. Posters for *Nobody's Home* had been tacked up on the bulletin boards.

"Actually, she's a sixth grader," Ben said, "but she placed into seventh-grade honors math."

"She must be really smart," Corey observed.

Ben nodded. "She is, but she's also shy, and sometimes she gets picked on. People make fun of her for loving math so much."

"She didn't seem that shy at rehearsal," Hannah remarked.

"I know," Ben said. "I noticed that too. She seemed more comfortable and confident than I've ever seen her."

"The theater must really suit her," Hannah said.

"Just like the lab suits me," Ben said.

He opened the door to the forensic science classroom, and they headed in together.

"Please take your seats," Miss Hodges said from the front of the room. "We have a lot to do. Today we're going to learn about paper chromatography."

Paper what? Corey thought. *This sounds complicated.*

"Don't be afraid of the word 'chromatography,'" Miss Hodges said, fiddling with the pencil in her hair. It was as if she'd read Corey's mind. "The 'chroma' part means 'color.' 'Graphy' is 'writing.' So chromatography is just color writing."

"Sounds more like art class than forensic science," grumbled Ricky Collins, a guy who liked people to think he was tough.

"Well," Miss Hodges said, "we might use chromatography to see if a piece of evidence from a crime scene matches a sample from a suspect."

Miss Hodges looked at her students, who were staring at her blankly, and smiled. "I see a lot of puzzled faces. Okay, let's take it one step at a time."

She explained how a person could take a piece of paper with a mixture on it and put it into a liquid. As the paper soaked up the liquid, the different parts of the mixture would make different colors on the paper. That could help an investigator figure out what substances the mixture was made up of or identify it.

"Let's try it," she said, bringing out beakers with liquid in the bottoms. "You can do this with all kinds of mixtures, but today we'll do it with ink."

The students broke into groups of three. Hannah, Ben, and Corey stuck together. Miss Hodges gave each group a piece of special paper (coffee filters cut into long strips) that had a dot of ink on it and three pens labeled 1, 2, and 3. At the top of the paper directly above the first dot was the letter A. Each group's job was to put three more dots of ink, from three different pens, horizontally across the paper. At the top of the paper, directly above each new dot, they wrote 1, 2, 3, to match the pen it came from. Then they had to carefully put their pieces of paper into the liquid.

Corey stared at the piece of paper in their beaker.

"Practicing mindfulness again?" Ben joked.

"I'm watching the four dots, but nothing's happening," Corey said. "Maybe we did it wrong."

"Miss Hodges said we have to give the liquid time to soak into the paper," Hannah said. "We just have to be patient."

"Not my favorite word," Corey complained.

He didn't have that long to wait, though. As the liquid soaked into the paper, the little dots of ink started to turn into lines of color.

Miss Hodges walked around the classroom to

see how each group was doing. "Look at the colors that appear on the paper. Are they the same as the original dots?"

Corey looked closer. The ink dots had looked as though they were just one color. But as the liquid traveled up the paper, the dots separated into different colors. What had looked like a solid black dot now had a blue part and a red part.

"Remember," Miss Hodges said. "When I gave you your paper, it had one original ink dot on it, labeled *A*. Which one of the ink dots you added is now showing the same color pattern as the original dot, *A*? Number one? Number two? Or number three?"

Every group got the right answer: number three. When they looked at the color patterns on the paper, it was easy to see that the color patterns of ink dot number three matched the color patterns of the original ink dot *A*. The original dot must have been made with pen number three.

"Cool!" said Ricky. His friends in the back of the class looked at him, surprised. "I mean, if you like that kind of thing," he added quickly.

"So I think you can all see that paper chroma-

tography can be very useful in helping an investigator decide what kind of ink was used to write a note found at a crime scene," Miss Hodges said. The students nodded in agreement.

"CSIs can also use paper chromatography for lots of other mixtures besides ink," she went on. "Even the dyes in candy."

Ricky cracked another joke. "Now a candy lab would make forensic science fun!" His pals laughed.

Corey didn't laugh, but his stomach did growl at the mention of candy.

Luckily, forensic science was followed by Corey's favorite period: lunch.

In the cafeteria, Ben, Hannah, and Corey decided to start their investigation by coming up with a preliminary list of suspects.

"I'm not sure about this," Ben said. "We really haven't done any investigating at all. Isn't it a little early to be listing suspects?"

"Normally, yes," Hannah said. "But in this case, it seems as though the circumstances narrow the list down right away. Whoever's trying to sabotage

Nobody's Home would need to know the script. . . ."

"And they're keeping the script secret," Corey said. "So the mystery won't be ruined."

"Right," Hannah agreed. "Also, the, uh . . . What's the word for someone who's committing sabotage?"

"'Saboteur'?" Ben suggested.

"'Jerk'?" offered Corey.

Hannah laughed. "Anyway, the person who's messing with the props would have to have access to the auditorium during rehearsals."

"So, access to the theater and access to the script," Corey said. "That means the five cast members, the stage manager, and the director. Seven suspects."

"What about the playwright, Theo?" Hannah wondered aloud. "He was there yesterday."

Ben and Corey thought for a moment. "I don't know," said Ben thoughtfully. "Kelly mentioned that yesterday's rehearsal was the first one he'd been to, and the props have been going missing for a while."

"Yeah, you're right," said Hannah. "We can cross him off our list."

Ben nodded reluctantly. "So our suspect list

makes sense, but we still need evidence. We need to investigate."

"I say we go back to rehearsal this afternoon," Hannah said firmly, "and keep a very close eye on each of the seven suspects."

"Sounds like more mindfulness!" Corey said.

Chapter 5

"D id the eyes in that painting just move?" Penelope asked.

Her brother Horace stood up. "Which painting?"

"That one," Penelope said, pointing. "The one of the ugly man."

"That ugly man," Horace said, "is our grandfather."

Corey, Hannah, and Ben were watching the rehearsal of *Nobody's Home* from the back of the auditorium. They tried to read the body language of the actors, to see if any of them seemed as though they might be guilty of sabotaging the play.

But it was tricky since the five students were playing roles. They weren't being themselves. The things they were saying were lines they had memorized. Their movements had been given to them by the director, Mrs. Gordon. And their faces were supposed to express the emotions of their characters, not necessarily their own emotions.

"Maybe we should be backstage," Corey whispered to Hannah and Ben, "watching the props."

"I'm not sure Mrs. Gordon will let us hang around backstage during the rehearsal," Hannah whispered back. "We might get in the way of the actors."

"I think the key is to carefully observe the suspects every time the rehearsal stops," Ben murmured.

"But the rehearsal hasn't stopped," Corey whispered a little too loudly. "And they're supposed to keep going no matter what!"

At the front of the auditorium, Mrs. Gordon turned around and glared. She was the only other person watching today. Theo hadn't shown up. Corey knew the junior varsity basketball team had practice every day this week for a game on Saturday afternoon.

Club CSI stopped talking immediately. They didn't want to get banned from the rehearsals. That might bring their investigation to a complete halt.

John, the actor playing the part of Horace, messed up several of his lines, but everyone kept going. He seemed distracted.

Ben wondered if John was nervous because he'd done something to jeopardize the play.

Tessa, who was playing the part of Millicent, crossed the stage and opened a closet door. She stepped into the closet, saying her line, "It might not have been a ghost you saw at all. It might simply have been someone wearing a sheet. Here, I'll show you."

But when she came back out of the closet, she wasn't carrying a sheet. She was just pretending to carry a sheet.

"Whoever was trying to make us think he was a ghost might have covered himself with a white sheet, like this," she said, pretending to cover her head with the sheet that wasn't there.

"He *or she*," Tim said in his role as Bernard.

"Hold!" Mrs. Gordon said. It was what she called out every time she wanted the actors to stop.

Tessa turned toward the seats in the auditorium. "But, Mrs. Gordon, I thought you said to keep going no matter what."

"I did," Mrs. Gordon said, standing up. "But we need to rehearse this scene with the sheet. Where is it? Courtney?"

The stage manager peeked out on to the stage.

"After rehearsal yesterday, I put the white sheet in the closet myself. Did you move it?"

Courtney shook her head. "No, Mrs. Gordon. I don't know what happened to the sheet."

Mrs. Gordon sighed. "All right," she said. "It couldn't have gotten far. Let's find that sheet before we continue." She climbed up the steps on to the stage and headed backstage to look for the missing sheet. The other cast members started searching the set, the wings (the offstage areas to the right and left of the set), and the backstage area behind the set.

Except for John.

He stayed on the set, plopping down into an easy chair. He pulled some sheets of paper out of his back pocket and studied them.

"Why isn't John helping to search for the missing sheet?" Hannah whispered.

"Maybe he wants to study his lines," Corey said. "He was messing up pretty badly before."

"Or maybe he isn't searching for the sheet because he already knows where it is," Ben suggested.

John didn't budge from the chair. Now and then he looked up from the sheets of paper he was studying, but he didn't look for the missing white bed sheet at all.

After a few minutes Mrs. Gordon came back onto the set. "Okay," she said. "I give up. I can't find the sheet anywhere."

"Neither can we," Melissa said, entering from the left wing.

"Any luck?" Mrs. Gordon asked the other cast members as they returned to the set. "Anyone?"

They all shook their heads. Even John, who hadn't looked at all.

"All right," Mrs. Gordon said. "We'll have to improvise." She turned to the stage manager. "Courtney, what do we have that we can temporarily use in place of the sheet? A blanket? A towel? A poncho?"

Courtney scurried backstage. They all stood on the set, waiting. In a couple of moments she returned carrying an old curtain. "Will this work?" she asked. "It's a little dusty."

"Ew," Tessa said. "I have to put that dirty curtain on my head?"

Mrs. Gordon took the curtain from Courtney. "This'll do fine, Courtney. Thank you." She shook the fabric a few times. Dust filled the air.

Kelly sneezed.

"Here, Tessa," Mrs. Gordon said, handing the curtain to her. "It's not dirty. Just a little dusty. Don't worry."

Tessa took the prop, looking totally worried.

"Put it in the closet, and we'll start from your line as you cross to the closet to get the sheet," Mrs. Gordon instructed, walking back down the steps to her seat in the auditorium. "By the way, from now on, at the end of a break like this, I'll just ask you to 'restore.' That means to go back to the last place we started, with yourselves and all the props and furniture put back in the positions they were in at that point."

Holding it at arm's length, Tessa carried the curtain to the closet, put it in place, and closed the door. Then she crossed the stage and waited.

"All right, Tessa," Mrs. Gordon said. "Go ahead."

Tessa said her line, crossed to the closet, and

took out the curtain. When she put it on her head, she acted as if its dustiness didn't bother her at all. That was good acting.

At the end of the rehearsal, the actors all sat on the edge of the stage, writing on the backs of their scripts as Mrs. Gordon gave them notes.

Like the day before, there were a lot of notes.

When she'd finished giving her specific comments, Mrs. Gordon looked up from her notebook to address the whole cast.

"Now, this is a general note for everybody. Let's be very careful with where we put our props. I'm tired of all these props going missing. You all need to step up your efforts a notch. We open Friday night. Today is Tuesday. I don't want you to embarrass yourselves in front of our first audience. Before tomorrow's rehearsal, make sure all your props are where they should be."

The cast members seemed discouraged. They stared at their scripts or drew little circles on the stage with their fingers.

The only one who didn't look crestfallen was John. He just looked distracted, as though he was thinking about something else.

"I think we need to talk to John," Ben whispered.

"Agreed," Hannah said. Corey nodded.

As the actors trudged out of the theater, Hannah, Corey, and Ben caught up with John. He looked lost in thought.

"John?" Hannah asked.

Startled, John turned around. "Yeah?"

"You're really good as Horace," Hannah said, smiling. She'd learned that it never hurt to start out with a compliment when you were going to question a suspect.

But John didn't smile back. "Thanks," he said, "but I'm not really sure about that."

"Have you got a second to talk?" Ben asked.

Melissa and Tessa passed by them, chatting.

John shook his head. "Nope. Gotta go. Sorry."

He turned and hurried out the doors. They slammed closed, and he was gone.

"That was weird," Corey said.

"John really didn't want to talk to us," Ben mused.

"Maybe it's me," Corey said. "I think I forgot to put on deodorant this morning."

He sniffed his armpits, then smiled. "Nope! Fresh as a daisy!"

Chapter 6

The next morning was a beautiful day in their small Nevada town, but the members of Club CSI were worried.

How were they going to talk to John?

As they walked to school together, they discussed possible methods.

"I think what we need is an interrogation room with bright lights and a one-way mirror," Corey suggested.

"I think you've been watching too many cop shows on TV," Ben said.

"Okay, fine," Corey said, picking up a rock and tossing it at a tree. *Whack!* Even though the tree had a narrow trunk, Corey nailed it. "Maybe we could find out what his favorite food is. Like, say, maybe it's ice cream. Then Hannah could invite him to an ice-cream place—"

Hannah looked annoyed. "I am *not* asking John out on a date!"

"Who said anything about a date?" Corey asked. "This is just a friendly trip to get ice cream."

"In other words, a date," Hannah said.

"There'd be nothing to worry about," Corey reassured her. "I'd be stationed in the corner, disguised as an ordinary ice-cream eater."

"This whole plan just sounds like an elaborate way for you to get ice cream," Ben said, laughing.

They were about a block from Woodlands Junior High School. That didn't give them much time to figure out a way to approach John.

But then John stepped out from behind a tree. Right in front of them.

"Hey," he greeted.

"Hey," Corey said. "We were just talking about you. Listen, do you like ice cream?"

Ben looked curious. "Were you waiting for us?"

John looked embarrassed. "Yeah," he said. "Sorry about yesterday. I wanted to talk to you guys, but I didn't want to do it around the other cast members."

"What did you want to talk about?" Hannah asked encouragingly.

John motioned for them to follow him. The four of them stepped behind the big tree where John had been waiting.

"I'm worried," he said, lowering his voice.

"What about?" Ben asked.

"That it's my fault," John explained.

Corey was confused. "That what's your fault?"

"All the stuff that's been going wrong with the play," John said. "All the missing props and everything."

"Why would that be your fault?" Hannah inquired. "Are you the one moving the props and sabotaging the play?"

John shook his head. He paused a moment, picking at the tree's bark. Then he took a deep breath and spoke quickly, as if he wanted to get it over with. "About a week ago, just before all these problems with the play started, I left my copy of the script in the boys' locker room."

Corey made a puzzled face. "Why?"

"I didn't do it on purpose!" John blurted. "I was carrying the script with me everywhere, so I could

learn my lines. I pulled it out of my backpack and then got distracted."

"By what?" Corey asked.

"I don't remember," John said. "Someone snapped a towel at me or something. That's not important. The point is, by the time I realized my script was missing, more than an hour had passed. And then by the time I found it, another hour had passed."

Ben leaned against the tree, thinking. "So you're afraid that while your script was sitting there in the locker room for two hours . . ."

"Someone copied it or took pictures of the pages," John said. "And then put it back."

"If somebody did that, someone who's not working on the play could know about all the scenes and the props and would be able to sabotage it," Hannah said. "This person might be sneaking into the auditorium and misplacing props."

John nodded. "Exactly," he said. "That's what I'm worried about. The more stuff that goes wrong at rehearsal, the more I think about it and the harder it is to concentrate on my performance. I keep messing up."

"In two hours, just about anyone could have

been in that locker room and done it," Corey said.

"Any *boy*," Hannah corrected.

Ben checked his watch. They needed to get going if they were going to be on time for homeroom.

"Do you have your script on you right now?" he asked.

"Yeah," John answered. "I haven't let it out of my sight since."

Ben pulled out a large plastic bag from his backpack and held it open. "Drop your script in here."

For the first time that morning, John smiled. "Do you always carry plastic bags with you?"

"Of course he does," Hannah said, grinning.

"You never know when you're going to encounter important evidence," Ben said.

"Or a sandwich," Corey added.

John dug his script out of his backpack and dropped it into the plastic bag. Ben zipped it closed.

"What are you going to do?" John asked. "Check it for fingerprints?"

"Exactly," Hannah said.

"Which means we'll need to take your fingerprints for comparison," Corey said as he shouldered his own backpack. "Meet us at the forensic science classroom at the beginning of lunch. It'll only take a second."

"Thanks," John said. "I'll see you then."

"Don't be late," Corey said. "We don't want to be late for lunch."

"Or homeroom," Hannah added. "Come on."

In the forensic science classroom, which Club CSI nicknamed "the lab," Miss Hodges was setting beakers on the tables. "Today we're going to continue working on chromatography. It's a big part of forensic science and definitely deserves more than just one class session."

Corey was relieved. Chromatography was pretty complicated, and he wasn't sure he'd grasped all the concepts in the last lesson.

"But instead of ink," Miss Hodges continued, "we'll be analyzing these." She turned a bag over and dumped leaves on the front table.

"My dad has me analyze those all the time," Ricky announced. "Only he calls it 'raking.'" His buddies at the back of the classroom laughed.

After watching Miss Hodges's demonstration,

Ben, Hannah, and Corey got to work doing paper chromatography on leaves. Following the instruction sheet, they pressed a green leaf down hard onto the same kind of chromatography paper they had used yesterday. The green pigment stuck to the paper.

Next they inserted the strips of paper into beakers with some rubbing alcohol at the bottoms, being very careful not to let the green pigment touch the alcohol, at first. As the alcohol soaked up into the paper and through the area with the green pigment, different colors appeared.

"This bottom band of color looks olive green," Hannah observed, jotting notes.

"But the band above it looks more blue green," Ben said.

Corey peered at the strip of paper hanging in the beaker. "Then there's a yellow band of color."

"And above that, it gets more orangish," Hannah reported.

Once everyone in the class had observed the different colors revealed by the chromatography, Miss Hodges wrote the names of the leaf pigments on the dry-erase board at the front of the classroom:

Blue green = chlorophyll a

Olive green = chlorophyll b

Yellow = xanthophyll

Orange yellow = carotene

Red = anthocyanin

"During the summer, when there's lot of sunlight, the leaves are full of chlorophyll, so they look green," Miss Hodges explained. "But when the weather changes in the fall, the leaves lose chlorophyll. The green goes away, and we see the other colors, like yellow and orange."

Miss Hodges tossed her dry-erase marker in the air and then caught it. "Now what, you may ask, does this have to do with solving crimes?"

Ricky raised his hand.

"Yes, Ricky?" Miss Hodges asked.

"What does this have to do with solving crimes?"

Miss Hodges raised an eyebrow and one side of her mouth. "Any ideas?"

Ben raised his hand, and Miss Hodges called on him. "It might help you match leaves from a crime scene to leaves on the shoes of a suspect."

"It also might help you figure out what time of year a crime happened, based on how much chlorophyll was left in the leaves," Hannah added.

"Excellent!" Miss Hodges said. "As the labs from the past two days should have shown you, paper chromatography is another very useful tool in the forensic scientist's kit, so it's important for all of you to understand it. Also," she added, winking, "it's sure to be on the next test."

After class, Hannah, Corey, and Ben found John waiting for them outside the lab. They took him to a deserted hallway, near the school's old trophy cases, to get his fingerprints.

"There," Corey said as John pressed his last finger onto a white card. "Now we just have to see if anyone else's prints are on your script."

"Can I watch you do it?" John asked.

"Well," Hannah said, "we'll do the analysis after school. Don't you have rehearsal?"

John nodded glumly. "Yeah, I do. But I doubt I'll enjoy it much."

Chapter 7

While John was not enjoying his rehearsal of *Nobody's Home* in the school auditorium, Club CSI was analyzing the fingerprints on his script in the empty forensic science classroom. Miss Hodges had given them permission to work in the lab. She had also taught them a new technique for finding fingerprints that weren't immediately visible.

"As always, just be very careful with any equipment you use," she said as she went into her tiny office. "If you need me, I'll be right here, grading the chromatography lab reports."

Ben carefully took the plastic bag holding the script out of his backpack. Then he put on plastic gloves and slipped the script out of the bag. Still holding the script by its edges, he looked around.

"Where should I put this?" he asked.

"Somewhere really clean," Corey said. "So I wouldn't suggest taking it to my bedroom."

Hannah spread clean aluminum foil on one of the lab tables. Then they divided the script into three sections. Each member took a section and then began to place the pages into plastic containers with iodine crystals inside. Then they covered the containers and floated them in warm water in the sink. The iodine quickly turned into vapor and, like magic, any fingerprints on the pieces of paper became visible.

"Hey," Hannah asked suddenly. "Are either of you reading the script? Because I don't think Mrs. Gordon actually wants us to know the ending."

Corey and Ben shook their heads. "We're too busy looking for fingerprints on the script to actually read the script," Ben said.

"Besides, reading the ending would ruin the play," Corey added. "And we're still going to opening night, right? I mean, we already paid for our tickets. And I don't think there are any refunds."

Once they finished exposing any fingerprints on

the pages of the script, they moved to the micro-scopes and started to examine the prints under magnification to see how many of them belonged to someone other than John.

But after careful examination they had their answer: zero.

"Every single one of these fingerprints belongs to John," Hannah said, sounding frustrated.

Ben took the stack of index cards and put them in an envelope. "I guess nobody took his script while it was in the locker room. It just sat there for two hours, and then he came back and got it."

"He'll be relieved to hear that," Corey said, dig-ging an orange out of his backpack and starting to peel it. "He seemed really worried that he'd ruined the play."

"Well, he may feel relieved," Hannah said, "but I feel frustrated. I was really hoping that a finger-print from John's script might lead us to a suspect."

Corey separated a section from his orange and offered it to Hannah. She shook her head. He popped the segment into his mouth, chewed, and swallowed.

"What about Mrs. Gordon?" Corey asked.

"What about her?" Ben replied.

"I mean, as a suspect," Corey said. "I was just thinking about the notes she gave at the end of rehearsal yesterday. She seemed really mad. And worried that the play might end up being embarrassing."

Ben looked confused. "I agree that she seemed upset. But I don't see how that makes her a suspect."

Corey stood up and paced around the lab, thinking. "Maybe she's unhappy with the play, so she's sabotaging it."

Now it was Hannah's turn to look confused. "Corey, that doesn't make any sense. If she's worried about being embarrassed by the play failing, why would she try to make it fail?"

Corey shrugged. "I'm just tossing out theories. Think of it this way: About a week ago, Mrs. Gordon realizes the play isn't going to be any good. In fact, it's going to be a huge failure. Which will make her look really bad, since she and the other eighth-grade English teacher are the ones who assigned their students to write a play, then picked out Theo's play to put on, then Mrs. Gordon cast it and directed it. If the play bombs, she's going to look like she didn't know what she was doing. Maybe she'll even get fired."

"I doubt she'd get fired for that," Ben said.

"So," Hannah said slowly, "you're saying Mrs. Gordon decided to sabotage the play herself, to make it look like someone was messing with the props. That way, it wouldn't be her fault when the played failed. It'd be the fault of whoever was messing with the props."

"Which is her," Corey said, nodding enthusiastically. "Only nobody knows it. And she pretends she doesn't know where the missing props are, even though she's the one who hid them."

"Hmm," Ben said, considering Corey's theory. "That's pretty out there, but I guess it's possible."

Miss Hodges stuck her head out of her office. "Pardon me for eavesdropping," she said apologetically. "I should have closed my door. I like to respect your privacy when you're working on an investigation."

"That's okay," Hannah said. She was always happy to hear Miss Hodges's opinions. "Did you hear what Corey was saying about Mrs. Gordon?"

"Yes, I did," Miss Hodges said. "And while I admire your thoroughness in considering every possibility, I really think you're headed down the wrong track with this one."

"Why do you say that?" Ben asked.

Miss Hodges leaned against the frame of her office door. "Because I've heard Mrs. Gordon talking about *Nobody's Home* in the faculty lounge. She really wants the play to succeed. It means a lot to her. She says the cast members have worked very hard, and they deserve to have a huge success in front of big, enthusiastic audiences." She laughed. "Every day she reminds us to buy tickets and to bring our friends and family to see the play. I bought my tickets weeks ago."

Ben grinned. "Well, that's pretty convincing. I think we can safely take off Mrs. Gordon from our list of suspects."

Hannah nodded in agreement. But Corey hated to completely give up on his theory.

"I don't know," Corey said. "I don't think we should eliminate her just because she's a teacher. Teachers can do bad things too. No offense," he added quickly.

Miss Hodges smiled. "None taken. And I'm not saying take her off the list of suspects because she's a teacher. I'm saying that based on what I've heard her say about the play, I'd put her at the bottom of your list."

By the time Club CSI finished their fingerprint analysis and hurried over to the auditorium, rehearsal was letting out.

John was one of the first cast members out of the theater, and Hannah took him aside. "We checked all the fingerprints on your script," she said, handing it back to him.

"And?" he asked nervously.

"Only yours," she said. "No one else has touched it."

John smiled, looking relieved. "So that means no one took it from the locker room and copied it?"

"Looks that way," Ben said. "If they did, they were wearing gloves the whole time. And that seems pretty unlikely."

"That's great," John said. "Thanks." He looked at his script. "I was kind of worried about not having my script to study today. But it was okay. I remembered all my lines. I guess I actually know them!"

"So we're fresh out of suspects," Hannah reported. "You don't know anyone who'd want to ruin the play, do you?"

John shook his head. He was grateful to Club CSI for reassuring him that no one copied his script, and he said he'd definitely think about it.

As the other cast members emerged from the auditorium, Corey noticed something weird. They were smiling. All of them.

Kelly ran up to Hannah. "Rehearsal went *so well*! We ran through the whole play, and no props were missing!"

"Really?" Hannah asked. "That's fantastic!"

"Maybe Mrs. Gordon was right," Kelly said. "Maybe everything that had gone wrong was just coincidence. And nerves."

The other cast members agreed. They were ready to call the case closed. They left the auditorium laughing and grinning.

"Maybe there never really was a case," Corey mused, watching them go. Hannah nodded.

"Maybe," Ben said, thinking. "Then again, tomorrow is their final dress rehearsal. If someone really wants to sabotage the play, that'll be their last chance."

"But what are we supposed to do about it?" Corey asked. "We can't watch the theater all night and all day."

"We can't," Ben said, "but a camera could."

Chapter 8

S o, you're saying we should set up a camera here in the auditorium?" Hannah asked, gesturing with her arms opened wide.

"Exactly," Ben said, folding his arms decisively.

Hannah and Corey thought about this. "Well," Hannah said, "I guess it couldn't hurt anything."

"Or cost anything," Corey added. "Except maybe batteries."

Hannah pulled out her phone from her bag and looked at it. "My phone has a video camera. But it would run out of charge."

"That's why we need a really good digital camera," Ben said. "One that's plugged in. And one with a lot of memory."

"Where can we get a camera like that?" Corey asked.

Ben smiled. "I just happen to know the president of the AV club," he said proudly.

"Are we supposed to be surprised that you know the president of the AV club?" Hannah asked.

"What's 'AV'?" Corey asked. "Anti-vegetable?"

"Audio visual," Ben explained.

"There's a club for that?" Corey asked.

"Come on," Ben said. "If we hurry, we can probably still catch Peter in the AV room. He usually stays late after school checking all the equipment."

Ben pulled on his backpack and started to go.

"Wait," Hannah said. "I'm not sure we can just set up a camera without permission. In fact, I'm not even sure we can *get* a camera without a teacher's permission. We should ask Mrs. Gordon."

Ben hesitated. He knew Mrs. Gordon didn't believe anyone was trying to sabotage the play. What if she said no? Then again he was pretty sure Hannah was right about needing permission.

"Okay," he agreed reluctantly. "Let's ask her."

They found Mrs. Gordon backstage putting props in place for the next day's run-through. Everyone else had left. She looked up, surprised to see the three students there.

"Yes?" she asked. "Did you need something?"

Corey believed in getting right to the point. "We want to put a camera in here overnight and during the day tomorrow," he said.

"Why?" Mrs. Gordon asked.

"So if anyone messes with the props, we'll have it on record," Corey explained.

Mrs. Gordon sighed. "I appreciate your trying to help make sure that *Nobody's Home* is a success. But I never did think anyone was trying to sabotage the play. And today's rehearsal went very smoothly—not a single missing prop."

"But what could it hurt to have a camera running?" Hannah asked. "If nobody does anything, then you're right. And if someone does do something, we'll see who it is. And then you'll be able to stop them before they ruin your opening night."

Mrs. Gordon thought a minute. "All right."

"Great!" Corey said. "Also, could you put that in writing so we can check out a camera?"

Mrs. Gordon laughed. "Fine. I'm an English teacher. I like putting things in writing."

62

Peter, the president of the AV club, carefully read every word of Mrs. Gordon's note.

"Well," he said. "She says you need a camera, but she doesn't say what for."

He wasn't sure he trusted these three seventh graders who'd come barging into the AV center so late in the afternoon. Peter was in eighth grade, and he took his position as the president of the AV club seriously.

"We need it for our investigation," Ben explained.

"Not a class?" Peter asked.

"No," Hannah said.

"Technically, I'm only supposed to release the equipment for class projects. There's also a form the teacher's supposed to fill out. She's not supposed to just write a note," Peter said, holding up the piece of notebook paper Mrs. Gordon had written on.

He didn't want to be mean or anything, but the AV equipment was worth a lot of money. Principal Inverno had stressed that when he put Peter in charge of signing it out.

Ben put on his friendliest face. "Right, but, unfortunately, we don't have time to get the form and have Mrs. Gordon fill it out. She's about to leave, and we need to set up the camera right away."

"For your investigation," Peter clarified.

"Right, for our investigation," Ben said, nodding.

Peter still stood there looking at the note, thinking.

"Look, can you either give us the camera or tell us to get lost, because I'm starving," Corey said, patting his stomach.

Peter laughed and pushed his black hair out of his eyes. "Okay, you can have a camera. But be careful with it. These cameras cost a lot of money."

He pulled out a set of keys and opened a closet door. Then he turned on a light, stepped into the closet, and came back out holding a small digital camera.

"Can we have a power cord, too?" Ben asked.

"And a tripod?" Hannah added.

"And a carrying case?" Corey chimed in. "A really cool one. Like, maybe black leather."

Peter sighed.

Back in the theater, Ben finished positioning the camera on the tripod. He'd set it up toward the

back of the auditorium, aimed at the stage. They had debated where best to put the camera. It was a hard decision to make because the props had gone missing from both backstage and the actual stage. In the end they decided that putting the camera at the back of the auditorium was best. This way they could see the whole stage *and* it would give them the best chance to capture anyone who might enter the auditorium when they weren't supposed to.

"There," Ben said, looking through the camera one more time. "You can see the whole stage. It'd actually be better to have several cameras."

Hannah grinned. "Oh, yeah, like your friend Peter would've given us several cameras. He parted with this one like it was his puppy."

"Don't exaggerate," Corey said. "We just have to remember to feed it, walk it, and clean up after it."

Mrs. Gordon came out from backstage and peered into the auditorium. "All done? I'm ready to go."

"All done," Hannah said. "If anyone messes with anything on this stage, we should catch it."

"And more important, we'll catch the culprit," Corey added.

Chapter 9

At lunch the next day, Corey, Ben, and Hannah were surprised to see John approaching their table with a tray full of food. "Mind if I sit down?" he asked.

"Not at all," Corey said. "Have a seat."

John sat down next to Ben.

"What's up?" Hannah wondered.

"Remember how you asked me to think about who might want to ruin our play?" John asked. "Well, I'm not sure anyone actually is trying to sabotage the play anymore, but I remembered something last night that might be useful."

He drank from a bottle of water, looking around to see if anyone in the noisy cafeteria was listening to their conversation.

"This might be nothing, and I don't want to accuse someone who's innocent," he continued, "but I'm in Mrs. Gordon's English class. And there's this kid in the class named Mark who was really jealous when Theo's play got picked."

All three members of Club CSI leaned forward. This sounded promising.

"He got an A on his play, but Theo got an A+. And I remembered that when Mark found out I'd been cast in the play, he said something to me about how it should have been *his* play that got chosen. He seemed mad about it." When John finished talking, he took a bite of his sandwich and chewed.

"That is interesting," Ben said.

"Very interesting," Hannah agreed.

"What does this Mark kid look like?" Corey asked. "Is he here in the cafeteria right now?"

John looked around. The cafeteria was crowded with kids laughing and eating. "There he is," John said. "On the other side of the room. Sitting by himself at that long table. He's got brown hair and a blue shirt."

Corey started to twist around in his seat to look.

"Don't be so obvious!" John hissed. "I really

don't want him to know I'm talking about him."

Corey slowly turned around, pretending to look down at the floor for something he'd dropped. Eventually, he looked up and across the room. He saw a brown-haired boy eating by himself, reading an English textbook. Ben and Hannah saw Mark too.

"I'm going to go eat with Tim," John announced. "We're running lines together."

"Okay," Hannah said. "Thanks for the lead. Break a leg at the final dress rehearsal this afternoon."

"Thanks," John replied, picking up his tray and walking away.

"That wasn't very nice," Corey admonished.

"What wasn't?" Hannah asked.

"Telling him to break his leg."

Hannah giggled. "That's how performers say 'good luck.'"

"Oh," Corey said. "Performers are weird." He stood up.

"Where are you going?" Hannah asked.

"To talk to our new suspect," Corey answered.

Ben held up his hands. "Wait, not so fast. Shouldn't we talk about this before we just run over and question him?"

Corey looked slightly exasperated. "Normally, yes. But the dress rehearsal is tonight. We might not get another chance to find out if Mark is the guy who's been ruining everything. Come on. Lunch doesn't last forever . . . unfortunately!"

Corey started to walk across the cafeteria. Ben and Hannah had no choice but to jump up and follow him over to the table where Mark was sitting alone.

"You're Mark, right?" Corey asked.

The thin eighth grader looked up from the textbook he was studying, surprised to see three seventh graders standing in front of him.

"Yeah," he said suspiciously. "Who are you?"

"I'm Corey, and this is Hannah and Ben. We're Club CSI."

Mark thought for a second and then nodded. "I've heard of you guys. You solve mysteries around school."

"That's right," Hannah said in her friendliest voice. "We thought maybe you could help us with something we're working on."

"Sure," Mark said, shrugging. "Whatever."

The three investigators sat down. Since they

hadn't had a chance to discuss the approach they were going to take with Mark, they weren't sure what to ask him first. Corey decided to get straight to the point.

"You're in Mrs. Gordon's English class, right?" he asked.

"Yeah," Mark said.

"Did you write a play for her class?" Corey continued.

Mark brightened a little. "Yes, I did. A comedy. Got an A, too."

"But she didn't pick your play to be the school play," Ben said, following Corey's lead. They might as well be direct.

"So what?" Mark said. "That doesn't mean it's not just as good. May be better."

"What do you think of *Nobody's Home*?" Hannah asked.

Mark shrugged again. "I don't know."

"Did you read it?" Corey asked.

Mark shook his head. "No. Why would I? I didn't audition or anything. I'm a writer, not an actor. And they're being pretty secretive about it. What's it about?"

The three investigators exchanged a quick look. If Mark didn't even know what the play was about, how could he have sabotaged it? And he sounded as though he was telling the truth.

"Are you going to see it?" Hannah inquired.

Mark frowned. "Nah. I'm really not interested."

"Not interested or too jealous to go?" Corey asked. Sometimes it worked to push people's buttons.

"Not interested," Mark said firmly. He shoved his book into his backpack and stood up. "Is this how you solved those other crimes? By asking a bunch of stupid questions?"

They were losing him. Corey decided to just go for it. "Did you mess with the props?"

Looking disgusted, Mark slung his backpack over his shoulder. "You mean the props for the show? No, I didn't mess with them. Why would I do that? Now, stop messing with me."

He walked away.

Ben looked at Hannah and Corey. "Well, what do you think?"

"His body language said he was telling the truth," Hannah said. "He didn't fidget, and he looked us right in the eyes."

Corey nodded. "I believed him."

"I doubt he could have faked telling the truth that well," Hannah added. "He said he wasn't an actor."

"He could have been acting when he said that," Corey suggested. Hannah shot him a look. "But, yeah, I don't think he was faking either."

Ben took in a long breath of air through his nose and then blew it out. "Agreed. He's jealous, but I don't think he did anything about it."

The question still was, did someone else?

After school that day, they had their answer.

Chapter 10

I t was the beginning of rehearsal. Ben was unplugging the digital camera when they all heard it.

A scream.

"Where'd that come from?" Hannah asked, looking around the theater.

Ben pointed toward the stage. "There!"

Corey was already running down the aisle toward whoever screamed. He didn't bother with the stairs. He jumped onto the stage and ran behind the set that had already been put in place for the first act.

He saw Tessa, the girl who played Millicent, standing with her hands covering her mouth. She was staring at the set for act two, which was set up behind the set for act one.

It was splattered with hot-pink paint.

On the wall of the dining room set, someone had used the hot-pink paint to write: MILLICENT DID IT.

"'Millicent did it'?" Corey read. "Did what?" He gestured toward act two's ruined set. "This?"

Shaking her head, Tessa said, "No. Not this. I play Millicent, and I certainly didn't do this."

The other cast members arrived, shocked by what they saw. "Why would someone do this?" Tim asked. "And why would they give away the ending?"

Ben and Hannah had followed Corey, and Ben asked, "You mean in the play it turns out Millicent is the one who's been trying to scare away the others?"

"Yeah," Tim said. "Whoever did this knows how the play ends."

Corey whispered to Hannah, "See? I told you one of the sisters did it. And you said that wasn't fair."

Hannah gave Corey a quick look that told him to drop it.

Mrs. Gordon walked in briskly. But when she saw the paint splattered all over act two's set, she slowed down and then stood there, staring.

The whole cast waited to see what she'd say.

"Well," she said. "It looks as though I was wrong. Someone has been trying to sabotage this play. And it's worked. I don't see how we can possibly fix the set in time for tomorrow's opening."

She shook her head, looking discouraged.

"What are we going to do, then?" John asked.

Mrs. Gordon took a deep breath. "We're going to cancel."

The five cast members started to protest, but Mrs. Gordon held up her hand. "I'm sorry," she said. "I know you've all worked very hard to be ready for opening night, and I'm proud of you. But the second act's set is extremely important in this play. We can't do the show without it."

"Will we put on the show on Saturday night?" Melissa asked. "My whole family's coming."

"I don't know," Mrs. Gordon said. "We'll have to see. Right now I think the important thing is to get out the word that the first performance is canceled due to . . . unforeseen circumstances. Courtney?"

The stage manager stepped forward. "Yes, Mrs. Gordon?"

"I'm putting you in charge of making signs

announcing the cancellation. The whole cast will help you."

"Right," Courtney said, nodding. "Come on," she said to the five cast members as she headed offstage. They followed her, looking miserable.

Ben, Corey, and Hannah stayed on stage, studying the ruined set. Ben knelt down for a closer look. Hannah was taking pictures with her phone's camera.

"Pictures are always a good idea, Hannah," Corey said. "But aren't you forgetting something?"

Hannah stopped taking pictures for a second. "What?"

"We had the digital camera running," Corey said. "We must have gotten video of the whole thing, including who did this."

Ben stood up and turned to face Corey. "I don't think so."

"Why not?" Corey asked, surprised. "We haven't even checked the recording yet."

Ben walked over and patted the back of act one's set. "Because of this," he said. "The set for act one. It was between the camera and act two's set, blocking everything. I doubt we caught anything."

Corey looked at the back of the damaged set. He saw what Ben meant. The way the scenery was set up, the wall with paint flung across it was invisible from the auditorium seats. And that meant it was invisible to the camera in the auditorium. He sighed.

"Well, I still think it's worth reviewing the recording," he said. "We might have caught *something*. Maybe the person who did this walked through the auditorium on their way backstage."

"I agree. We should always be thorough with any evidence, no matter how unlikely it is that we'll find something," Ben said. "And speaking of evidence, I want to get a sample of this hot-pink paint."

He knelt down by the splattered wall again. Opening his backpack, Ben dug out a plastic bag and a metal scraper. Carefully, he removed some of the dried paint from the set, put the evidence into the plastic bag, and sealed it.

While Ben gathered his paint sample, Hannah and Corey searched the set and the backstage area for any additional evidence.

"Do you see any open cans of paint or used paintbrushes?" Corey asked. "Maybe we could find some fingerprints or shoe prints."

"Nope," Hannah reported, checking the corners of the backstage. "Whoever did this must have taken everything away after they messed up the scenery."

Corey stared at the big, bright pink letters on the dining room wall: MILLICENT DID IT. "Why do you think the saboteur decided to spoil the ending?" he asked.

"I think it was to make sure the set couldn't be used," Hannah said. "If there were just random blotches of paint, they might have been able to quickly paint over it in time for the opening night's performance. It probably would have been hard to cover up such a bright color of paint, but if it was only squiggles and doodles bleeding through, it might not have mattered. But there's no way you could do the second act of the show with the name of the culprit coming through and showing up on the wall."

"That makes sense," Corey conceded. "Wow. I guess whoever did this *really* didn't want them to perform *Nobody's Home*."

"I guess not," Hannah agreed.

"Do you think we could do handwriting analysis on this?" he asked, peering at the pink message.

"I kind of doubt it," Hannah said. "It looks as though whoever wrote this used a paintbrush. Painting with a brush isn't like writing with a pen. And they probably tried to disguise their writing, anyway. They knew they were doing something really wrong."

Ben put on his backpack. "Come on. Let's go to my house. We can check the camera's recording on my laptop."

"How long will that take?" Corey asked, shouldering his own backpack.

"The camera was on for hours," Hannah said. "It could take a long time."

"In that case," Corey said, "we'd better stop and pick up some snacks."

Chapter 11

Ben's room was full of scientific equipment: microscopes, beakers, chemistry sets, and test tubes. The walls were covered with posters related to science. One showed the periodic table of the elements. Another pictured different species of whales. There was a big black-and-white photo of Albert Einstein sticking out his tongue.

Ben's mother kiddingly called his bedroom "the lab." Ben secretly liked that.

"I love what you've done," Corey joked.

"What do you mean?" Ben asked, puzzled. "It's the same as the last time you were here."

"Okay, then I love the nothing you've done," Corey corrected himself. He started to dig out the snacks they'd bought on their way to Ben's house.

Hannah plopped her backpack onto Ben's bed. "Let's get going on reviewing the recording," she said. "I'm afraid it'll take all night, and I've got homework."

Ben took the memory card out of the camera and then pushed it into his laptop's SD slot. "You're probably right," he said. "I've got homework too. Maybe we should watch the footage in shifts. One of us could watch the screen for twenty minutes while the other two work on their homework. Then we could switch."

"Good idea," Corey said, biting into an apple. "You go first."

While Hannah and Corey opened their textbooks and started doing their homework, Ben watched the first twenty minutes of the recording.

It wasn't very interesting.

A single light was shining onstage. (Mrs. Gordon told Club CSI it was called the "ghost light," but she didn't tell the cast members that, since she also knew there was already a rumor about the theater being haunted.) Act one's set was set up.

No one came. Nothing moved. Watching the recording was like staring at a painting.

After twenty minutes, the alarm on Ben's phone went off. He paused the playback, rubbed his eyes, and reached for his homework.

"Anything?" Hannah asked, even though she was pretty sure Ben would have spoken up if he'd spotted anything.

Ben shook his head. "Nope. Nothing."

"Okay, well, I'll go next," Hannah offered.

"Have fun," Ben said, opening his math book.

Hannah did not have fun. Staring at the unchanging recording of an empty stage was about as interesting as watching a tree grow. Actually, less interesting. With a tree, at least the occasional leaf blew in the breeze.

When Corey's turn came, he made a suggestion less than a minute into his shift. "I say we fast-forward through this."

Ben looked up from his homework. "But we might miss something."

"I don't think so," Corey said. "Nothing is moving. In fast-forward, we'll be able to spot someone coming onto the stage without any trouble. The person'll stick out like a sore thumb."

After thinking about it, Ben and Hannah agreed.

Corey hit the fast-forward button. At first he was only watching it at double speed, but soon he had it up to fifteen times the actual speed.

The picture on the laptop still looked pretty much like a painting. The light flickered a little bit, but nothing moved.

"I wish a mouse would at least run across the stage," Corey complained.

"So you wish our school was infested with mice?" Hannah asked, grossed out.

"I didn't say 'infested,'" Corey said. "I said 'a mouse.' Or even a bug. Like, maybe a big beetle or something. Or a bat. Anything!"

They decided that if all three of them watched the computer screen, they could run the fast-forward at its top speed.

But there was nothing. They came to the end of the recording. The last thing they saw was Ben walking up to the camera and turning it off. And they'd seen nothing suspicious.

"So whoever smeared paint on the set was hidden behind act one's set the whole time," Hannah said. "Where the camera wouldn't catch them. They must have come in through the side stage door."

"That seems right," Ben said, disappointed. Even though he'd thought act one's set would block the act of vandalism, he'd hoped maybe they'd spot something. Even a quick glimpse of the saboteur might help them figure out who they were.

"Maybe the Mad Paint Splatterer knew about the camera," Corey suggested.

Hannah shook her head. "Only Mrs. Gordon knew. And I'm sure she didn't do this."

"That's why I set up the camera where the audience would be," Ben said. "That way it wasn't nearly as obvious as if I'd set it up onstage. Now I wish I'd put it somewhere backstage, maybe hidden in a corner."

"There's no way you could have known ahead of time what the best angle would be," Hannah said. "And we only had one camera."

"Which we have to return to Peter first thing tomorrow morning," Ben said, stretching. It was almost dinnertime. "We'd better call it a night."

The next morning Ben, Hannah, and Corey headed for the AV club's room in the learning center to

return the equipment Peter had loaned them.

They passed posters that announced *Nobody's Home* was opening that night. But now all the posters had pieces of paper taped across them saying CANCELED.

Hannah kind of felt as though Club CSI had failed. If they'd figured out who was messing with the props earlier, they could have stopped the person before they ruined the set. And they still didn't have any good leads to follow!

Peter looked up from a tangle of power cords when Club CSI walked in. "I wish people would return these cords coiled up," he complained. "It's really a pain having to untangle them."

Ben felt relieved that he'd made a point of carefully coiling the power cord they'd borrowed. He handed the carrying case to Peter. Peter unzipped it and then smiled when he saw everything neatly arranged in the black leather case.

"So, did you catch the bad guy?" he asked.

"No," Corey said. "The only thing I got out of watching our recording was a stiff neck."

Ben explained to Peter what they'd done with the digital camera, setting it up in the theater and letting it run to try to catch the culprit.

"But when we reviewed the recording, we didn't see anything," Ben concluded.

"Except for the set," Corey said. "Boy, did we see that. And see it and see it . . ."

Peter thought for a moment. Then he had an idea. "You watched the recording, but did you *listen* to it? Sometimes what can't be seen can be heard."

All three investigators shook their heads. "We had it on fast-forward most of the time, so we didn't hear the audio," Hannah explained.

"Then I'd suggest listening to the soundtrack," Peter said. "Maybe you'd catch something that way."

Corey looked discouraged. "You mean we should go through that boring recording *again*?"

Peter smiled. "I could help you. Got any free periods today?"

It turned out Ben and Peter had a free period in common. They agreed the two of them would come back to the AV room and see what they could find out.

"Or rather *hear* what we can find out," Ben said.

Later that morning Ben returned to the AV room. Peter was already there, fiddling with some equipment.

"We'll play back the recording on this computer," he said, patting an old desktop.

Ben looked skeptical. "What'll the sound be like?"

Peter grinned. "It'll be great. Because we're going to run the audio from the recording through this."

He then patted a black piece of equipment on a shelf. It looked like some kind of amplifier.

"The sound will come out through those," he said, pointing to a pair of large speakers hanging in the corners near the ceiling.

Ben nodded. "Sounds good."

"Oh, it'll sound better than good," Peter said. "It'll sound excellent."

Peter was right. When they played the recording, the sound that came through the speakers was crisp and clear. They could even fast-forward the recording and still hear the sound, though it was sped up.

Through most of the recording the sound was very consistent—a kind of unchanging hum.

"That's probably just electrical equipment in the auditorium," Peter guessed.

"Makes sense," Ben agreed. "There are a lot of lights, and a big electrical box to control them might hum even when all the lights are turned off."

"Except for that one light," Peter noted.

"Right," Ben said.

They continued to watch the playback in silence.

But then they heard something different.

Peter stopped the recording and rewound it a little. Then he turned up the sound and played back the recording at its normal speed.

"Hear that?" Peter asked, excited.

"Yes," Ben said. "Definitely. It sounds like a door opening. And then footsteps."

"Yeah," Peter said. "You're right. But what's that other sound?"

There *was* something else. Over the footsteps, another sound could be heard. A higher sound. Familiar, but they couldn't quite place it.

What could it be?

Chapter 12

After his free period, Ben had forensic science. He could hardly wait to tell Corey and Hannah about the sounds he and Peter had heard on the recording. He hurried through the crowded halls of Woodlands Junior High.

He spotted Hannah and Corey ahead of him in the hallway, heading toward class. "Hannah! Corey!" he called. His two friends turned around, but no one else even noticed him yelling. Everyone was noisy between classes—talking, laughing, squealing, banging their locker doors . . .

Hannah hurried to Ben. "So, did you hear anything on the recording?"

Corey was right beside her. "Like maybe someone saying, 'I did it! I'm the Mad Splatterer!'"

Ben laughed. "Nothing quite that conclusive. But Peter and I did hear something interesting."

The three of them stepped around a corner into a slightly quieter hallway where they could hear one another without having to shout. Ben told Corey and Hannah about the sounds of the door opening and the footsteps. And the jingling sound he couldn't identify.

"Very interesting," Hannah said. "Did you happen to notice what the recording's time stamp said when these sounds occurred?"

"Definitely," Ben said. He consulted a small notepad he always carried with him. "It was just before seven a.m. The sound of the door opening happened at six fifty-seven a.m."

"Could you be a little more precise?" Corey joked. "How many seconds after six fifty-seven was it?"

Corey looked at Hannah to see if she thought his questions were funny. When Corey teased Ben, Hannah was usually his best audience. But right now she seemed horrified.

"What's the matter?" Corey asked. "Is that the time the theater ghost always appears?"

Hannah shook her head slowly. "No," she said.

"But I think I might know who ruined the set."

"Who?" Ben asked.

"Kelly," Hannah said reluctantly.

Corey looked confused. "Why do you say that? Just because Ben heard a door open really early in the morning?"

"Because I know Kelly gets to school really early in the morning," Hannah explained. "Her parents have to be at work at seven, so they always drop her off at school when it opens at six forty-five. Every day she's one of the first students to arrive. She'd have time to sneak into the auditorium and destroy the set way before she had to be in homeroom."

Ben looked doubtful. "I don't know. Other students get here early too. And the saboteur might have come in early just to wreck the set, even if they don't usually get here so early in the morning."

"Besides," Corey pointed out, "Kelly's the one who brought the case to us in the first place!"

Hannah ran her fingers through her hair. "That's true," she said. "But maybe the cast asked her to bring in Club CSI because they knew she was friends with me. She didn't want to make them suspicious by refusing, so she agreed to ask us. She didn't think we'd end up figuring out she was the one trying to stop the show."

"Well, we could check out that possibility pretty easily," Ben said. "We'd just have to talk to one of the other cast members and see if they asked Kelly to approach us about investigating."

Hannah frowned. "I hate suspecting Kelly. She's my friend. If she's innocent, I want to find out as soon as possible. Why don't we talk to her at lunch today? Maybe we'll be able to figure out whether she was at school early yesterday morning."

"Sounds good to me," Corey said. "I always like a plan that includes lunch."

Carrying their trays, Ben, Hannah, and Corey headed toward their usual table in the cafeteria. Ben and Corey sat down, but Hannah set down her tray on the table and remained standing, looking around the cafeteria for Kelly.

"There she is," she said, spotting her across the room. "I'll invite her to eat with us."

"Excellent," Corey said. "While you do that, I'll start eating." He bit into his sandwich with gusto.

"Hey, what happened to mindfulness?" Ben asked.

"I'm saving it for our investigation," Corey said with his mouth full. "I don't want my mind to get *too* full."

Moments later, Hannah returned with Kelly. Ben and Corey looked for signs of guilt on her face. All they saw was sadness.

Hannah pulled out a chair for Kelly. "We just thought maybe we could talk a little bit about our investigation."

Kelly looked even gloomier. "What's the point?" she mumbled. "The play's canceled."

"Permanently?" Corey asked.

Kelly pushed the food on her tray around with a fork. "I'm not sure. But it doesn't look good. Mrs. Gordon has at least canceled the shows for this weekend." She looked up from her lunch. "It's so unfair. We put in so much time rehearsing. I've been working really hard on this play."

Ben decided to get to the point of the interview. "Kelly, were you here at school early yesterday morning?"

She didn't even have to think about it. "Yeah," she said. "I'm always here early."

Hannah looked worried. Could her friend have ruined the set? Was she just pretending to be upset about the canceled performances? In rehearsal she'd seemed like a pretty good actress. . . .

"And I had to be here early yesterday morning, anyway," Kelly continued, "because I met with Mrs. Gordon in her office."

Hannah looked surprised. "Mrs. Gordon? Why?"

"To go over my lines," Kelly said. "I've danced in lots of recitals and even ballets, but I've never been in a play before, and I was nervous about blowing my lines on opening night. So she agreed to practice my lines with me before school."

Hannah felt much better. If Kelly was with Mrs. Gordon first thing in the morning, then she couldn't have been in the theater making the sounds Ben had heard on the recording.

They assured Kelly that they'd do everything they could to help the play go on. She thanked them and then went back to sit with her friends.

"So that settles that," Hannah said. "Kelly was with Mrs. Gordon."

"Just to be superthorough," Corey said, "we should check her alibi."

Just before the end of the lunch period, Hannah, Ben, and Corey found Mrs. Gordon in her office, grading quizzes. She looked up and smiled when she saw who was standing in the doorway.

"Hello, crime scene investigators," she said. "Did you catch anything on your camera?"

"Nothing definite," Ben said, "but we might have something to follow up on."

Mrs. Gordon sighed. "Well, I guess that's better than nothing at all. Though I'd hoped you'd see who ruined the set, so we could stop all of this."

"We were just wondering if we could ask you something," Hannah said.

"Of course," Mrs. Gordon replied. "What would you like to know?"

"Did you help Kelly go over her lines yesterday morning?" Corey asked.

Mrs. Gordon raised her eyebrows. "Yes, I did."

"What time?" Ben asked.

The teacher thought a moment. "From about ten to seven until nearly seven thirty."

Hannah was relieved. Kelly's alibi checked out.

"Why do you ask?" Mrs. Gordon inquired.

Ben hesitated. He didn't like to give out information from an investigation while it was still ongoing. "We're not sure," he said vaguely. "But it might turn out to be important." He decided to change the subject. "Are you going to cancel the play completely?"

Mrs. Gordon frowned. "I'm still thinking about that. We're not performing *Nobody's Home* this weekend, but after that, I'm not sure. I'm going to talk to the principal this afternoon and then let the cast know after school what we've decided."

Chapter 13

Ben and Hannah stood outside the auditorium, waiting for Corey after school.

"Where is he?" Hannah fretted. "I don't want to miss Mrs. Gordon's announcement."

"Here he comes," Ben said, spotting Corey running down the hallway toward them.

He sprinted up and then stopped. "Sorry I'm late. I wanted to make sure it was okay with the basketball coach if I missed the beginning of practice again to go to the rehearsal."

"This isn't a rehearsal. It's just an announcement," Hannah said. "Come on. Let's go in."

She opened the heavy double doors, and they hurried into the theater. Mrs. Gordon was standing on the stage. The five cast members and the stage manager were sitting on the furniture used in the first act. Hannah, Ben, and Corey slipped into seats close to the stage, so they could hear.

"Thanks for coming," Mrs. Gordon said to the cast. "I wish I was giving you a speech about how great your opening performance is going to be tonight. But, as you know, there was just no way we could have fixed the set in time. You've worked very hard on the play, so I'm really sorry we've had to cancel your big opening night, as well as this weekend's performances, just because of someone's malicious behavior."

The cast members and the stage manager all looked unhappy. They stared at the floor or up into the space above the stage.

"But," she continued, "I have some good news."

That got the students' full attention. They looked right at Mrs. Gordon. Good news?

"This afternoon I spoke to Principal Inverno, and we agreed that the show should go on."

The cast members smiled, then broke into applause and cheers. Mrs. Gordon smiled too, but held up her hands for them to quiet down.

"Instead of canceling the play completely," she

said, "we're just going to postpone it for a week. That'll give us time to rebuild the set for the second act. The principal managed to find some money in the school's arts budget to pay for the new set."

"You mean there's actually money in the arts budget?" Tim asked. That got a laugh.

"Just a little," Mrs. Gordon admitted. "It'll take all of us working together to rebuild the set in time, but I know we can do it."

The cast cheered again.

"But I'm afraid that's going to mean working tomorrow, even though it's a Saturday," Mrs. Gordon said. "Is that all right?"

They all cheered a third time, though maybe not quite as loudly.

Corey turned to Hannah and whispered, "Does that mean *we* have to be here on a Saturday too?"

Hannah nodded. Corey slumped down in his seat and sighed.

"I'll bring brownies," Hannah said. Corey brightened and sat up straight.

As Mrs. Gordon and the cast members figured out what time they'd meet on Saturday to work, Club CSI watched them closely. Did anyone seem as though they were trying to hide their guilty feelings? Did anyone seem disappointed that the play was going to be performed after all?

No. No one seemed as though they were feeling any of those things. Everyone seemed happy *Nobody's Home* was going to be postponed instead of canceled. And everyone seemed pretty cheery about coming in on a Saturday to help rebuild the set for the second act.

Club CSI didn't seem to be any closer to catching the culprit than they had been the first day Kelly had asked them to investigate.

The cast members gathered up their scripts and backpacks and then headed out, walking down the steps into the audience and then up the aisle toward the exit. They were talking and laughing, relieved and excited that all their hard work was going to pay off after all.

Club CSI stood up to follow them out. "So," Corey said. "About these brownies. Will there be fudge? Or nuts? Because I say, why not both?"

Suddenly Ben noticed something.

He heard a sound. A familiar sound.

When Courtney walked by Club CSI as she headed

up the aisle, the keys clipped to her jeans jingled. As stage manager, she had a bunch of keys to keep track of—keys to the auditorium, the prop closet, the dressing rooms, the lighting booth . . .

And the sound of those jingling keys was the sound Ben and Peter had heard on the recording. He was sure of it.

Ben gripped Corey's arm to get him to stop talking.

"Ow," Corey said. "What?"

Ben raised a finger to his lips. "Listen," he whispered.

Corey and Hannah froze, listening carefully.

"All right, time to go!" Mrs. Gordon called from the stage. "I'm afraid everyone needs to clear out. See you tomorrow!"

Courtney was gone. Ben turned back to Mrs. Gordon. "Okay, Mrs. Gordon. See you tomorrow. What time are you starting?"

"Eight a.m.," she answered. "Bright and early."

Corey groaned quietly. "There goes my Saturday morning sleep."

Once they were out of the theater, Hannah asked Ben, "What was that all about? What were we listening for? I didn't hear anything unusual."

Ben looked around. He wasn't sure whether or not Courtney was still inside the school. "Let's not talk here. Let's go to the park."

The park was just a couple of blocks away, but by the time they got there, Hannah was about ready to burst.

"Okay!" she said to Ben. "We're at the park! Talk!"

Ben took off his backpack and sat down on a bench. He unzipped his bag and pulled out his Quark Pad. A while back he, Hannah, and Corey had each received an expensive Quark Pad from the company that made them as a thank-you for their help in discovering a ring of thieves who were stealing them. They all loved their Quark Pads . . . and the tablets always came in handy when they were working on a case.

"I heard it," he said. "In the theater. I heard the mysterious noise Peter and I found on the recording from the morning the set got ruined. That's why I had you listen. I wanted to see if you heard it too."

"The only thing I heard was my stomach growling," Corey said, pulling out an apple from his backpack and biting into it. "And speaking of growling, Coach'll be really mad if I don't get to practice any second now."

"What was it?" Hannah asked. "What did you hear?"

"As Courtney walked past us, I could hear all those keys on her key ring jingling," Ben said, pulling up the audio file. "When I heard that, I realized it was the same sound I heard on the recording. I copied the recording onto my Quark Pad. Listen."

Ben clicked on the play triangle and turned up the volume. Hannah and Corey leaned in close to hear. First they heard a door open. Then footsteps. And then . . .

"Keys jingling!" Corey exclaimed. "So Courtney's our jerk!"

"No," Ben said, "she's our suspect. We don't really have any strong evidence yet that she's our saboteur. But she *is* our suspect."

"Our *lead* suspect," Hannah added firmly.

"Our *main* lead suspect," Corey called over his shoulder as he ran off to practice.

Chapter 14

Saturday morning was chilly. "Brrr," Hannah said as they walked up the school steps. "I should have worn a sweater."

"Forget the sweater," Corey said. "Where are those brownies?"

"What brownies?" Hannah asked innocently.

Corey pointed at the plastic container she was carrying. "Those brownies," he said. "The ones you're carrying. The ones I should be eating right now."

"Didn't you just have breakfast?" Ben asked as he opened the door.

Corey snorted. "Yeah, but there was hardly time for anything. All I had was a bowl of cereal, some fruit, juice, and a piece of toast." He thought for a second and continued, "Two pieces. Oh, and some yogurt."

Hannah shook her head as she handed him the brownies. "How do you stay so skinny?"

"Sports, I guess," Corey said. "I burn a lot of calories. Plus, I try to go easy on sweets." He pried the lid off the container. "Ah! Fudge!"

"And nuts," Hannah added.

"You're the best!" Corey declared as he lifted a gooey brownie to his mouth.

Inside the theater, Mrs. Gordon, the cast members, and Courtney were already onstage. It was kind of weird seeing the English teacher in her Saturday clothes—jeans and a T-shirt.

"Okay," she began, referring to her clipboard. "The first thing we need to do is pull the light fixtures off the old set."

"So we can repaint it?" John asked.

Mrs. Gordon shook her head sadly. "No, I'm afraid we're going to have to rebuild it. We can't risk having the solution to the mystery bleeding through the new paint. That'd ruin the surprise."

"Mrs. Gordon?" Ben asked, raising his hand. "Can we help too?"

"Absolutely," Mrs. Gordon said. "More hands make lighter work."

"We brought brownies," Hannah said.

"Then you're even *more* welcome," Mrs. Gordon said, smiling.

"We're sharing?" Corey asked Hannah, surprised.

"Yes. How many did you expect to eat?" Hannah asked him.

"All of them?" Corey mumbled.

As they headed toward the stage, Corey whispered to Ben, "Why are we going to help build the set? I thought we were just here to observe our lead suspect."

"I want to get close enough to really see what's going on," Ben said. "And hear what everyone's talking about."

They climbed the stairs to the stage and pitched in, helping to take off the light fixtures from the ruined set, which used to be an elaborate dining room in the mansion.

It was chilly inside the theater, too—almost as chilly as it was outside. Tessa went into the dressing room and then came back wearing a cardigan.

Then Hannah noticed something.

The cardigan had small paint stains on it. Hot-pink stains. And no one had started painting anything yet.

Hannah really wanted to examine the sweater more closely. Luckily, as Tessa worked on taking the set apart, she warmed up. Eventually, she took off the cardigan.

"Do you mind if I borrow your sweater?" Hannah said, rubbing her arms. "I'm freezing."

"I don't mind," Tessa said. "But it's actually Courtney's. I found it in the dressing room, and she said I could borrow it."

"Oh," Hannah said calmly, hiding her excitement from learning that the sweater belonged to their chief suspect. "I'll ask Courtney if it's okay for me to wear it."

Tessa smiled. "I'm sure she'll say yes."

Hannah carried the cardigan over to Courtney, casually hiding the paint stains in the folds of the material. The stage manager was kneeling on the floor, removing a screw from a board.

"Um, Courtney?"

She looked up. "Yes?"

"Would it be okay if I borrowed your cardigan?"

Hannah asked. "It's kind of cold in here."

"Sure," Courtney said, turning back to the two-by-four. "I keep that old sweater in the dressing room for just this sort of thing. You never know when they are going to blast the air-conditioning in here."

"Thanks," Hannah said. She walked away, acting as though she were in no big hurry, even though she felt like running.

Hannah picked up her backpack and slipped into the nearest bathroom, locking the door behind her. She carefully hung the cardigan on a hook. Then she dug through her backpack.

I must have an evidence bag in here somewhere, she thought.

Finally, in the last pocket, she found a small plastic bag. Perfect.

Using a hair clip she found in her bag, she managed to scrape off some of the pink paint from the cardigan into the bag. She didn't want to remove too much or Courtney might notice. On the other hand, why would Courtney leave incriminating evidence out in plain sight? She must not have realized the paint was on her sweater or, Hannah thought,

maybe it was just a coincidence and she had nothing to hide. They'd have to figure out a way to find out.

Hannah sealed the evidence bag and zipped it into her backpack's smallest pocket. Then she put on the cardigan. It was too small. Hannah was taller than Courtney, who was only in sixth grade. She was taller than Tessa, too, who was in seventh grade, but was one of the youngest seventh graders at Woodlands. Hannah's arms stuck out of the sleeves. She looked ridiculous.

She took off the sweater. Actually, she didn't want anyone noticing the paint stains, anyway.

She went back to Courtney. "You know, as I'm working, I'm warming up. Thanks, though." She held out the sweater. "Should I just hang your sweater back in the dressing room?"

Courtney didn't even look up from the task she was concentrating on. "Yeah, that'd be great."

Hannah took the sweater into the dressing room and hung it up, making sure the pink splotches were out of sight. While she was there, she looked around to see if she could find any more evidence of Courtney's guilt, but she didn't see anything unusual.

Still, she had the paint chips in her backpack, and that was something.

She came out of the dressing room and saw Corey helping John and Tim lower the dining room wall to the floor of the stage.

"Heads-up!" John called out. "The wall's coming down!"

After the guys brought down the wall, the other cast members got to work taking it apart. They could use the boards behind the set to build a new dining room.

Hannah picked a moment when everyone was busy to take Ben and Corey aside.

"I think I've got a good, solid piece of physical evidence," she whispered. She told them about the paint on Courtney's sweater.

Ben smiled. "That's great. We can analyze it in the lab on Monday. Maybe Miss Hodges will help us."

"Did Courtney say anything interesting?" Hannah asked.

"No," Ben said. "I tried to work close to her, so I'd be sure to hear everything she said, but she doesn't really say much. Just stays quiet and does her work."

"Well, you said before that she was shy," Corey pointed out.

"Yeah, but I thought she seemed more outgoing when she was working on theater stuff," Ben said. "Maybe I was wrong."

"Or maybe now she's just trying to be invisible," Hannah said. "If you'd done what we suspect she's done, would you want everyone talking to you?"

"So now that we have some evidence, how much longer are we going to stay here helping with the set?" Corey asked.

Ben thought a minute. "We should probably work a while longer and then leave separately. If we leave too soon, Courtney might suspect that we have what we need and that we're on to her."

"Why?" Hannah asked Corey playfully. "Don't you like building sets?"

"It's all right," Corey said, "but the brownies are all gone."

Chapter 15

Ben, who was usually an excellent student, had trouble concentrating in his classes Monday morning. He kept thinking about analyzing the paint samples after school. Would the paint from Courtney's sweater match the paint on the ruined set?

At the end of forensic science class, Hannah asked Miss Hodges if Club CSI could use the lab after school.

"No problem," Miss Hodges said.

"And will you be around, in case we could use a little help?" Hannah added.

"Oh, I'll be around," the teacher answered cheerily. "Between grading lab reports and planning lessons, I'm always around after school."

After the bell rang at the end of his last class, Ben zipped through the halls to the forensic science classroom. Miss Hodges let him in, and Hannah and Corey showed up seconds later.

"So, what are you working on today?" Miss Hodges asked.

"Paint samples," Ben said, digging through his bulging backpack. He pulled a plastic bag out of a pocket and held it up. "I scraped these off the ruined set. Have you got the samples from the sweater, Hannah?"

She pulled out the plastic bag of hot-pink paint flakes from her backpack and held them up. "Got 'em."

"We want to compare the two sets of paint samples to see if they match," Corey explained.

Miss Hodges nodded. "Did you notice if they used water-based or oil-based paints for the sets?"

"Actually, I did," said Ben. "They used water-based paints. Why?"

"That's great. We can probably do an experiment on it," answered Miss Hodges. She laid a yardstick across the middle of a table. "But first, I'd recommend setting up two separate work areas.

It's very important to make sure you don't mix the two samples."

Ben set his plastic bag on one side of the yardstick, and Hannah set her plastic bag down on the other side.

They began by comparing the colors of the two samples. To the naked eye, they seemed to match.

Next they transferred small flakes from each sample to glass slides and then examined them under microscopes. Again, they seemed identical.

"I think we have a winner," Corey said as he peered through a microscope.

"I think we could use more proof," Ben said.

Just as he said that, Miss Hodges emerged from the supply closet carrying a beaker and a container of water. "Recognize these?" she asked.

Corey nodded and smiled, looking satisfied with himself. "They're those things from that thing we did."

Hannah laughed. "Could you be a little more specific?"

"The thing with the leaves and the ink spots last week," Corey said. "Paper . . . something."

"Paper chromatography," Ben said.

"Yes. Exactly," Corey said, smiling slyly. "Just testing you."

Hannah helped Miss Hodges pour a small amount of alcohol into two beakers. Ben cut strips of paper from coffee filters.

"Since you've already done paper chromatography with leaves and pens, you're well on your way to becoming experts," Miss Hodges said.

"Yes," Ben said, "but with paint samples, wouldn't it be better to do pyrolysis-gas chromatography?"

Corey stared at Ben. "Wow," he said. "How does your tongue manage to wrap itself around those words without getting all cramped up?"

Miss Hodges smiled. "I'm impressed, Ben. I take it you read up on different methods of chromatography."

Ben nodded. "When we learned about paper chromatography, I saw how useful it could be in our Club CSI investigations. So I decided to learn a little bit more about chromatography."

"By reading, like, a whole book on it?" Corey asked. "Or a series of books?"

Ben made a face. He wasn't *that* nerdy. He hoped. "No, just an article. Or two."

"Well, to answer your question," Miss Hodges said, "yes, with paint, it could be better to do pyrolysis-gas chromatography. But, tell me, Corey, what do you think the 'pyro' in 'pyrolysis' means?"

Corey wasn't thrilled about being quizzed. When they were in forensic science class, Miss Hodges was their teacher. But when they were in Club CSI, she was supposed to be their faculty advisor.

Still, he was pretty sure he knew the answer.

"A pyro is someone who loves fires," he said confidently.

"Well, yes," Miss Hodges said. "'Pyro' can be short for 'pyromaniac.' 'Pyro' means 'fire.' In pyrolysis-gas chromatography, we use fire, or very high temperatures, to break mixtures down for analysis."

"How high?" Hannah asked.

"Oh, as high as six hundred to one thousand degrees Celsius," Miss Hodges answered.

"That's pretty hot," Corey said. "Even for Nevada."

"And it's much too hot for a school laboratory," the teacher continued. "There are real safety issues with pyrolysis-gas chromatography. It can only be done in a professional lab. So even though our results won't be quite as detailed, since this is

water-based paint, we're going to use paper chromatography on your paint sample. Much safer."

Corey remembered something from the first day of forensic science class. "Miss Hodges, don't you have a cousin who works at a crime lab in Las Vegas?"

"That's right," she said. "Good memory, Corey."

"Is there any possibility that he could do that pyro-gas thing for us?" Corey asked. "In the police crime lab?"

Miss Hodges thought about this. "Well, perhaps," she said slowly. "But we'd have to send the samples to him, wait for him to get a free moment, and then have him send us his results. It could take two to three weeks. Can you wait that long?"

The three friends looked at one another. If *Nobody's Home* was going to open successfully next weekend, they needed to solve this case and stop the saboteur as soon as possible.

"I think we'd better just go ahead with the paper chromatography," Ben said. "We don't have two weeks."

"Yeah," Corey said. "I agree. Besides, as Miss Hodges said, when it comes to paper chromatography, we're practically experts."

Working together, Club CSI and Miss Hodges mashed small chips from the paint samples into powder. Then they used the powder to paint dashes onto the strips of coffee filter paper. The pink pigment stuck to the paper.

"We'll do this twice," Miss Hodges said, "so we have a backup."

After Hannah had rubbed the pink powder onto two strips of paper, Ben carefully hung them in the beakers with one end barely touching the water in the bottom of the beakers.

"Make sure the paint isn't touching the water," Miss Hodges reminded him.

"It's not," he assured as he clipped the tops of the papers to pencils resting across the mouths of the beakers.

"Okay," Corey said. "Now we wait. My specialty . . . not."

While they waited, Miss Hodges went into her office, and the three friends tried to distract themselves with homework, but they couldn't help sneaking glances at the beakers every couple of minutes. The pink powder was starting to inch its way up the papers, separating into different colors as it rose.

Finally, Miss Hodges stuck her head out of her office and said she thought they could go ahead and compare the chromatograms.

The patterns of colors on the coffee filter strips were identical. The two paint samples matched!

"Looks as though Courtney's our culprit!" Corey said. He shook Ben's hand. "Congratulations on solving another mysterious case. You couldn't have done it without me. Should we go tell Mrs. Gordon?"

"Maybe we should run our evidence past Miss Hodges and see what she thinks," Hannah suggested. "Since she's right here."

Corey and Ben agreed. They asked Miss Hodges to come out of her office and hear what they'd discovered in their investigation. Ben told her about the jingling sound on the recording and how it had sounded just like the keys on Courtney's key ring. Hannah told her about finding the pink paint stains on Courtney's sweater and how they'd matched the paint on the ruined set.

"So that proves it. Courtney's our jerk." Corey stated.

"He means saboteur," Ben said.

Miss Hodges looked doubtful.

"Uh-oh," Corey said. "I think I know what that look means."

"You've done a good job of investigating this case so far," Miss Hodges began, "but I don't think you're quite ready to make an accusation."

"Why not?" Corey asked. "All the evidence points to Courtney."

"Well, you're suggesting Courtney is the one who's been vandalizing the props and the set. But it seems to me that there are other explanations for your evidence."

"Such as?" Ben asked.

"Just about anyone could have jingling keys," Miss Hodges said. "Especially if they needed keys to get into the theater early in the morning."

"That's true," Hannah admitted.

"And as for the matching samples of pink paint," Miss Hodges continued, "do you know if pink paint was originally used to paint the set, before the vandalism?"

Corey, Ben, and Hannah were quiet for a moment as they concentrated. They tried to remember if there was any pink on the set before it was vandalized, but they weren't sure. They shook their heads.

"If there was, Courtney might have gotten that same hot-pink paint on her sweater when she was helping to paint the sets in the first place," Miss Hodges said.

"And she did call her sweater 'old,'" Hannah piped up. "It's a shame she didn't tell me she'd just bought it, after they'd finished painting the set. Then it wouldn't matter if there was hot-pink paint on the original set."

Reluctantly, Corey nodded. As usual, their forensic science teacher was right. But he hated to admit it. He'd really thought they had the case all wrapped up.

"Sorry to burst your bubble," Miss Hodges said.

"That's okay," Hannah said. "We want to be sure we're right before we accuse anyone."

Yeah, Corey thought, *but how are we going to make sure we're right?*

Chapter 16

A s they walked out of the forensic science lab, the members of Club CSI were feeling gloomy.

"I still think Courtney did it," Corey said.

"But Miss Hodges is right," Hannah insisted. "We don't have enough proof to accuse her."

Ben was thinking. "At least we know that the two paint samples match. . . ."

"Yes, but Courtney may have gotten pink paint on her sweater while she was painting the original set," Hannah reminded him.

"Right," Ben said. "But did she? That's what we need to find out. Let's go to the theater. They're still building the new set for act two, aren't they?"

"I think so," Hannah said.

"Then come on," Ben said, quickening his step.

Hannah and Corey had to hurry to keep up with him.

When they got to the auditorium, the door was propped open.

And they could smell paint.

Inside, the whole cast, Courtney, and Mrs. Gordon were painting.

Ben walked quickly down the aisle of the theater and climbed the steps to the stage. "Mrs. Gordon, may we talk to you for a second?"

"Certainly," she said, carefully setting her brush on the edge of a paint can. She stood up and led the three investigators into one of the dressing rooms backstage, shutting the door behind them.

"What would you like to know?" she asked.

"We were wondering if we could check the original sets to see what colors of paint were used on them," Ben said.

"You can check act one's set," Mrs. Gordon said. "But all the painted parts of act two's set are gone."

"Gone?" Corey asked, dismayed. "On Saturday it seemed as though you were using the materials from the original set to build the new set."

Mrs. Gordon nodded. "Yes, we did use the two-by-fours. But they weren't painted. The walls—what we call 'the flats'—were the only painted parts. And we couldn't use those, so we put them in the trash."

"Any chance the flats are still out in the trash?" Hannah asked hopefully.

"I'm afraid not," Mrs. Gordon said. "The garbage men hauled away the trash early this morning."

That was discouraging. Now they could never get samples from the original set for act two.

"Is any of the paint left around?" Ben asked. "Hot-pink paint?"

"No," Mrs. Gordon said. "I know because I checked before we started painting the new set. I had to buy all new paint. That was one of the reasons I needed additional funds from Principal Inverno."

They were hitting nothing but roadblocks. Still, Ben had one more idea. "Was pink paint used on the set for the first act?"

Mrs. Gordon cocked her head and thought. "I don't think so. But you're welcome to look," she said, gesturing back toward the stage.

Trying not to attract the attention of Courtney or the cast members, the three friends went back onstage and thoroughly examined act one's set.

There was no pink paint on it.

"That's good," Ben said to Hannah and Corey quietly. "But we still don't know about the original set for act two."

They stood there for a minute, thinking. Then Corey's face lit up. "I've got it," he said. He hurried back over to Mrs. Gordon, who was just dipping her paintbrush back into the can of paint.

"I'm sorry, Mrs. Gordon, but could we ask you just one more favor?" he asked, putting on his friendliest face.

Mrs. Gordon sighed. "All right," she said, "but if we're going to be ready to open this Friday, I really can't have too many more interruptions."

She led them back into the dressing room. "Do you have a contact sheet for all the cast members with their e-mail addresses?" Corey asked.

"Yes," she said.

"May we have a copy of it?"

Mrs. Gordon hesitated.

"It's really important for our investigation," Corey said. "And unless we figure out who's been messing with your show, we won't be able to stop them from doing it again."

"All right," Mrs. Gordon said, reaching for her

notebook. "I originally made copies for everyone in the cast, and I've got a couple of extras." She pulled out a sheet and handed it to Corey.

"Great! Thanks," Corey said. He turned to Hannah and Ben. "Come on. Let's go."

They followed Corey out of the theater, mystified.

When they got outside, Ben spoke first. "All right," he said. "I admit it. I'm stumped. How is a list of e-mail addresses going to help us? We already know who's in the cast."

Corey smiled, pleased to have stumped Ben. "We'll e-mail all the cast members without telling Courtney. In the e-mail, we'll ask them if they have pictures of the set before it was messed up."

"I get it," Hannah said. "Then we'll closely examine their photos to see if there was any matching pink paint on the original set."

Ben nodded. "That is an excellent idea."

Corey made a slight bow. "Thank you."

"Come on," Ben said. "We can use my computer."

He hurried off down the sidewalk. Corey looked at Hannah. "Since when is *he* the one who runs everywhere?"

Chapter 17

S ince it was his computer in his room, Ben sat at the keyboard typing the e-mail to the five cast members.

But that didn't stop Corey and Hannah from making plenty of suggestions.

"Tell them not to mention this to Courtney," Corey said. "We don't want her to get suspicious."

"Yeah, but we also don't want to accuse Courtney yet," Hannah said. "So tell them not to mention this to *anyone*, since this is part of an ongoing investigation."

"Tell them that if their pictures are blurry, don't bother sending them, since that'll just slow us down," Corey suggested.

"But it doesn't matter if *people* in the picture are

blurry, as long as the *set* is in focus," Hannah added.

As he kept typing, Ben sighed at all these suggestions. Hannah noticed.

"Sign it 'Love, Club CSI,'" she joked.

"With hugs and kisses," Corey added, laughing.

When Ben had finished writing the e-mail, he sent it off to the five cast members, stressing how important it was for them to send back their photos of the set as soon as possible. Since all the cast members had their own phones, pictures started coming back almost immediately.

All five actors had snapped at least one or two pictures of the set with their phones. Melissa had taken dozens of shots. Ben put them all together in one big folder (which was in another even bigger folder devoted to the *Nobody's Home* case).

"Hey, I just thought of something," Corey said. "What about our recording of the set? Shouldn't we look at that?"

"You can't see act two's set on the recording," Hannah said. "It was blocked by the set for act one. Remember?"

"Oh yeah," Corey said.

Ben opened the photos one by one, zooming in

on each part of the set, looking for anything that might be painted pink. Hannah and Corey leaned in close, staring at the computer's screen. Among the different actors' pictures, they were able to examine the entire set.

There was nothing pink on the original set. Which meant Courtney hadn't gotten hot-pink paint on her sweater while innocently painting the original set.

"Makes sense," said Ben. "After all, the set is the inside of an old mansion. I don't know how much hot-pink paint they used back in the day."

"So we were right in the first place!" Corey said triumphantly. "Courtney got that pink paint on her sweater when she trashed the set. She *is* the jerk!"

"Saboteur," Ben corrected.

"Same thing," Corey said, shrugging.

The next day Club CSI told Miss Hodges about their photographic analysis.

"Well, this does seem to indicate a very strong possibility that Courtney did vandalize the set," she agreed.

"Should we confront Courtney?" Corey asked.

"She's just a sixth grader, so it's not like it'd be scary or anything."

"I think it'd be better for Mrs. Gordon to talk to Courtney," Miss Hodges said. "Why don't you go to Mrs. Gordon with your evidence and then suggest that she discuss your findings with Courtney herself?"

That sounded like a good idea.

In her office on Tuesday morning, Mrs. Gordon held the two strips of coffee filter paper Ben had pulled out of an envelope and handed to her.

"What am I looking at, exactly?" she asked.

"Chromatograms," he said. "It proves that the hot-pink paint from Courtney's sweater matches the hot-pink paint on the vandalized set. See how the color patterns are exactly the same?"

Mrs. Gordon nodded.

He set his Quark Pad on her desk. "And then there's this," he said, clicking on the play triangle.

Mrs. Gordon listened to the recording of a door opening, footsteps, and jingling keys.

"Ben noticed that when Courtney walks, her keys

jingle," Hannah said. "And they sound just like that."

"So she was the one in the theater that morning, ruining the set with pink paint that she accidentally got on her sweater," Corey said.

Mrs. Gordon shook her head, looking unhappy. "I don't understand it. Why would Courtney try to ruin the play? She loves theater, and she's worked so hard on *Nobody's Home*."

"We were hoping you would ask her that," Corey said.

Courtney sat on a chair in Mrs. Gordon's office, staring at the floor. Mrs. Gordon spoke to her gently.

"Can you explain these things, Courtney?" she asked. "The recording of the jingling keys? The pink paint on your sweater?"

Courtney held her mouth in a tight line. Then she took in a deep breath and blew it out.

"Yes, Mrs. Gordon," she said in a small voice. "I can explain the keys and the paint. I can't lie anymore. I did it. All of it. I took the props and I messed up the set with paint. I'm really sorry."

She kept staring at the floor, sitting very still.

"I thought you loved working on the play," Mrs. Gordon said.

"I do," Courtney replied.

"And you are such a good stage manager," added Mrs. Gordon. "Why would you do something like this?"

Courtney swallowed back tears. "Because . . . I had to."

"Why would you have to ruin the show?"

The sixth grader sat there for a minute, thinking, still staring at the floor. Then she looked up. Mrs. Gordon was facing her, but she didn't look mad. She looked really nice, as though she was just trying to understand. Courtney really liked Mrs. Gordon, who was always kind and fair to everyone.

It was time to fess up to the truth. The whole truth.

Chapter 18

B lackmail?" Hannah asked, astonished.

Mrs. Gordon nodded. "That's what she said. That someone was blackmailing her. That's why she had to try to stop the play."

Club CSI had come to Mrs. Gordon's office to find out how her meeting with Courtney had gone. They were very surprised by what the English teacher had learned.

"Who was blackmailing her?" Corey asked.

"She doesn't know," Mrs. Gordon said. "The threats were made in notes and e-mails. No one ever talked to her directly."

"But what could anyone possibly blackmail Courtney for?" Ben asked, amazed by this new information. "She's in my advanced math class.

She never gets in trouble for anything."

"Does *anyone* ever get in trouble in advanced math?" Corey asked him.

"Well, not really," Ben admitted. "We're all pretty into the math. But Courtney's especially polite and quiet."

"It's always the quiet ones," Corey said knowingly. "You know, unless it's the really loud ones. They can be trouble too."

Hannah thought the two boys were getting away from the main point. "So, what was Courtney being blackmailed for, Mrs. Gordon? Did she say?"

The English teacher nodded and sighed. "Courtney may be an excellent math student, but she's been having a lot of trouble in gym class. She was worried about her grade, so she cheated during her physical fitness test. She noticed that the gym teacher had written them in pencil in his grade book. She got her hands on the grade book, erased her actual scores, and rewrote in better scores. The gym teacher never noticed, but someone must have and decided to use that information against her."

"You mean she was so afraid her gym teacher

would find out she'd cheated that she was willing to ruin the play?" Hannah asked.

"Yes," Mrs. Gordon said. "Grades are extremely important to Courtney. I think she gets a lot of pressure from her parents to bring home an excellent report card. She's terrified that if her gym teacher finds out she cheated, he'll fail her and she'll have to take sixth-grade gym again next year."

Ben stood up and started pacing around the small office. He really wasn't even aware he was doing it. Sometimes walking helped him think.

"All right," he said. "So someone found out Courtney had cheated on her gym test. They sent her notes and e-mails threatening to tell her gym teacher if she didn't sabotage *Nobody's Home*."

"That's what she told me, yes," Mrs. Gordon said.

"So she did it," Hannah said, taking up the thread of Ben's summary. "She hid props so no one could find them. As the stage manager, she had easy access to all the props and knew which ones were the most important to the action of the play."

"Except for that one rehearsal," Corey remembered. "Last Wednesday. The last rehearsal before the morning someone wrecked the set. On Wednesday

Courtney didn't mess with any of the props. How come?"

"I asked her about that," Mrs. Gordon said. "She said she hadn't heard from the blackmailer for a few days, so she started to think maybe the whole thing had been a prank. But that night she received a very threatening e-mail."

"What did it say?" Hannah asked.

"I wrote it down," Mrs. Gordon said, looking through the papers on her desk. "Here it is: 'Perhaps you don't believe me, but my threat is real. Your gym teacher will be told. You have to stop the play. Or else!'"

"May we have a copy of that?" Ben asked.

"Of course, you can have this," Mrs. Gordon said, pushing the paper across to them. "The black-mailer's threat worked. Courtney was so scared that she finally did something that would halt the play, once and for all. She snuck into the auditorium the next morning and splattered the hot-pink paint all over the set."

"Why'd she write 'Millicent Did It' on the wall?" Corey asked.

"She knew having the ending revealed would

be a real problem for the production," Mrs. Gordon said. "She also knew hot-pink paint would be hard to paint over. The message would keep bleeding through. Courtney's very bright."

"Did she happen to say where she got the hot-pink paint?" Ben asked.

"Yes, I asked about that, too," she said. "Courtney said it was the last can of paint left in the supply room. The rest of the paint had been used up, but nothing on the set had been painted hot pink. After she wrecked the set, she got rid of the can of hot-pink paint, throwing it away in a trash can far from school. She didn't realize she'd gotten some on her sweater."

Mrs. Gordon smiled for the first time. "She was pretty amazed by your chromatography analysis. In fact, I'd say she was impressed."

She turned around and picked up a script and a piece of paper on the table behind her. "Courtney thought you might be interested in some more evidence, so she gave me these to pass along to you."

Hannah took the script and the piece of paper. It was a handwritten note.

"That's the first note the blackmailer sent to

her," Mrs. Gordon explained. "It was slipped into her locker. And this is Courtney's script, with all her markings to help her do her job as stage manager. She thought they might be helpful."

"Helpful for what?" Corey asked. "The case is solved. Courtney did it."

"And she's apologized. Profusely. But now that we know Courtney did it, we need to find out who *made* her do it," Mrs. Gordon said. "I'd say Club CSI has a new case. A case of blackmail."

As they walked home from Woodlands Junior High after school, Hannah, Ben, and Corey discussed the new turn their case had taken.

"I still don't really understand why Courtney sabotaged the play," Hannah said. "She loves theater. Why didn't she just go to a teacher or the principal when she got the first mean note?"

Corey bounced a tennis ball on the sidewalk and caught it as they walked. "What I don't understand is why she cheated on her test in the first place. Who cares if you get a bad grade in gym?"

Hannah reached over and caught the ball.

"Have you ever gotten a bad grade in gym?"

"Of course not," Corey said.

"Then you don't know what it's like," Hannah said, tossing him the tennis ball.

"It can be tough when your parents expect you to get straight As every time," Ben said. His own parents expected excellent grades from him, but they never punished him if he got a B. Although, come to think of it, he didn't remember ever getting a B.

"It's not just the bad grade," Hannah pointed out. "It's the shame of getting caught cheating. That could feel terrible. Courtney must have been really scared. I actually feel sorry for her."

"So do I," Ben said. "I've noticed after math class that sometimes Courtney gets bullied in the hallway by seventh graders. It's hard standing up for yourself when you're used to being bullied."

"Really?" Corey asked, catching the ball behind his back. "Now we're getting somewhere. Maybe one of these bullies is the blackmailer. "

They walked on, thinking about the possibility.

"I don't know," Hannah said slowly. "You said these bullies were seventh graders, right, Ben?"

Ben nodded. "Yeah, they were."

"But Courtney's in *sixth-grade* gym," Hannah observed. "So none of the bullies would be in gym with her. How could one of them have found out about her cheating on her test?"

That was a good question. Corey didn't have an answer.

"Still," Corey said, "I think the bullies are worth checking out." He turned to Ben. "We're not talking really big bullies, are we? I mean, they're seventh graders like us, right?"

"Yeah," Ben said. "They're not huge. And maybe one of them somehow found out about Courtney's cheating, even if they weren't in the same class with her. It's possible."

"But why would one of these bullies want the play ruined?" Hannah asked.

Corey shrugged. "Maybe they hate theater."

"Okay, so what's our next move?" Hannah asked.

"Do we know any of the bullies who have been bothering Courtney?" Corey asked.

"Not really," Ben said. "But I know someone who does."

Chapter 19

R icky Collins sat on the living room floor playing Zombie Monster Attack, his favorite video game. His mom wouldn't be home from her job as the head of his school's cafeteria for at least half an hour. When she came in, she'd tell him to do his homework before dinner. But for now, he could play the game.

He would have liked to have turned up the volume, but his dad, who worked nights at a bakery, was still sleeping.

Ricky guided his survivor through the smoldering ruins of a town. Just a few zombies left, and then he'd make it to the next level—the farthest he'd ever gotten.

Ding-dong.

Ding-dong?

Someone was at the door. He was tempted to just ignore it. But what if it was his mom? Maybe she forgot her key or something.

Ricky paused the game, got up off the floor, and walked over to the front door. When he looked through a window, he saw Ben, Hannah, and Corey from his forensic science class.

What were *they* doing here?

"What do you dorks want?" Ricky asked as he flung open the door.

"Hey, Ricky," Ben said in his friendliest voice. "We just thought maybe you could help us with an investigation."

"How do you even know where I live?" he asked. "It's not like I ever invited you over."

"We came over that time we were investigating the meatloaf mystery, remember?" Corey reminded Ricky brightly.

Ricky scowled. Hannah thought maybe that wasn't the greatest thing for Corey to bring up. Ricky had been pretty mad at them that time, since they'd treated his mother as a suspect.

"Anyway," Hannah said, wanting to change the

subject, "we thought maybe you could help us find out something."

Ricky sat down on the front stoop. Even though he liked to act tough, he was actually intrigued. He secretly liked the idea of doing an investigation. He watched a lot of crime shows on TV, and he thought he might even want to be a cop someday (though he never told anyone that).

"Like what?" he asked, pretending to be totally bored.

The three friends took turns telling Ricky about all the things that had gone wrong with the school play. They explained how they'd figured out Courtney was ruining the play. And finally they told about how they'd learned she was being blackmailed.

"Blackmailed?" Ricky repeated, surprised. "That's messed up. Who's blackmailing her?"

Corey sat down on the front stoop too, even though there wasn't a lot of room. "That's what we're trying to find out. And that's where you come in."

"Me? How?" Ricky shifted away from Corey.

Ben thought about sitting down, too, but there really wasn't room for a third person, so he just leaned on the handrail. "Well, after our math class together, I've noticed some seventh graders bullying Courtney in the hallway."

"Seventh graders from your math class?" Ricky asked.

"No, just some random seventh graders," Ben said. "But for some reason they keep picking on Courtney. I think one of them is named Zack."

Ricky looked offended. "Oh, and you think because I'm a goofball in class that I know every bully in school. Well, I'm not a bully. I just like to kid around. I'm really more of a . . . comic." When he wasn't thinking about being a cop someday, Ricky thought maybe he'd try being a stand-up comic.

"Do you know Zack?" Corey asked.

Ricky smiled a sly smile. "Yeah, I know him," he admitted.

"And his friends?" Hannah pressed.

"Yeah, I know them, too," he said. "They're all right. They just like to mess with people."

"Well, we were wondering if one of them might have written the notes and e-mails to Courtney," Ben said.

"We don't know those guys, but you do," Corey

added. "So we thought maybe you could talk to them and try to find out if one of them did it."

Ricky stood up and stretched. "I guess I could do that. But why should I?"

Hannah looked Ricky straight in the eyes. "You know, you say you're not a bully, but a lot of people think you are. So maybe if you did something helpful now and then, they'd stop thinking that."

Ricky almost got mad. Almost. But then he thought about what Hannah was saying. It made sense. And if he was going to be a cop someday, he'd have to get information out of people without them even knowing it. Maybe he could practice on Zack and his pals. It might be interesting.

A couple of blocks away Ricky's mom was trudging along the sidewalk toward home. She'd be there in a couple of minutes, and he wanted to go inside and save his video game before she arrived.

"Okay, whatever," he said. "I'll talk to Zack. And his buddies."

"Try not to let them know what you're doing, though," Ben cautioned.

"Duh," Ricky said. "I'm not an idiot."

He started to go inside.

"Thanks," Hannah said. "We appreciate it. Maybe sometime tomorrow afternoon you can tell us what you find out."

Wham. Ricky had slammed the door.

The next day at school Ben was hurrying to his next class when he noticed Ricky in the hallway. He was talking to Zack and his pals, laughing and joking around. Ben certainly didn't want to give away the fact that Ricky was helping Club CSI, so he steered clear of the group, avoiding eye contact with Ricky.

At lunch Ben told Corey and Hannah what he'd seen.

"That's a good sign," Hannah said. "It sounds as though Ricky was getting information from them."

"Or figuring out a way they could all be bigger bullies together," Corey said.

"Aw, Ricky's not so bad," Hannah said.

"I'm not? Thanks!" Ricky said, grinning. He'd come up behind them in the noisy cafeteria without them noticing.

Hannah blushed. To cover her embarrassment, Ben quickly asked, "What'd you find out?"

Ricky looked around. "We should meet some-where else. I don't want to be seen talking to you nerds. Bad for my reputation."

Corey, Ben, and Hannah looked offended. Ricky laughed. "I'm kidding! But Zack's right over there, and I don't want him to accidentally overhear us."

"You know the old trophy cases?" Corey asked. "Near the gym?"

Ricky nodded.

"Meet us there for the last ten minutes of lunch period," Ben said.

"The last five minutes," Ricky said. "I want to enjoy my lunch. And it won't take long to tell you what I found out."

The trophy cases at the end of the hall were dusty, with glass smeared by kids' fingers. Inside were old sports trophies with names of long-forgotten stu-dent athletes engraved on them.

Corey sat on the floor, tossing his tennis ball against the wall and catching it. Ben paced around, while Hannah peered into one of the trophy cases. Lunch period was almost over.

"He's not coming," Corey said. "He was messing with us."

"I don't think he'd do that," Hannah said.

"He said he likes to kid around," Corey countered. "Since when are you such a big fan of Ricky Collins, anyway?"

Before Hannah could answer, Ricky came sauntering down the hallway.

"So, what did you find out?" Ben asked immediately.

"They didn't do it," Ricky said. "End of story."

"How do you know?" Corey said. "You didn't ask them directly, did you? 'Cause I'm sure the blackmailer would lie."

Ricky looked annoyed. "Of course I didn't ask them directly. That'd be really dumb."

"Then what makes you so sure none of them blackmailed Courtney?" Hannah asked.

Ricky looked up at the ceiling as though he were trying to pick the perfect words. He always enjoyed having an audience.

"It's just not their style," he said.

"'Not their style'?" Corey repeated. This didn't seem very convincing.

"Dude, those guys aren't blackmailers," Ricky explained. "That'd take way too much effort and . . . imagination. It just wouldn't occur to them. Trip you in the hall? Yeah. Make fun of your hair? Sure. But blackmail you? No way."

"Did you talk to them about what's been going on with the play?" Ben asked.

Ricky laughed. "Yeah, I did. Those guys have no idea there even *is* a school play. 'What school play?' Those were their exact words. And I believe them."

Hannah, Ben, and Corey exchanged a look. They each knew what the other two were thinking. If Zack and his friends knew nothing about *Nobody's Home*, they certainly had no motive to blackmail Courtney into sabotaging the production.

Ricky turned and walked away. Without turning around he said, "Sorry, guys. Looks like you hit a dead end."

As they watched Ricky strut down the empty hallway, all three investigators thought the same thing: *He's right*.

Chapter 20

After school that day, Ben, Corey, and Hannah walked together to Ben's house. Usually when they were together, they talked nonstop.

But not today.

All three of them were thinking about what to do next.

"We could talk to Courtney ourselves," Corey suggested, but without much enthusiasm. "All we know is what Mrs. Gordon told us she said."

"We could, I guess," Hannah said. "But I doubt she wants to talk about it. She's probably ashamed of what she did. She told a teacher because she had to, but she might not want to talk to us at all."

They walked on for half a block in silence.

Then Ben said, "Let's go back to the evidence."

"What evidence?" Corey asked.

"The two pieces of evidence Mrs. Gordon gave us," he said. "Courtney's copy of the script and the first note the blackmailer sent her."

"Sounds good," Hannah said. "Your house?"

"My house," Ben said, nodding.

Anyone who had looked in Ben's room that afternoon would have seen a strange sight.

Three seventh graders were sitting on Ben's floor, staring at a script. Every once in a while, all three would look up, one by one. Then they'd nod, and Ben would turn the page.

They'd decided to read through the whole script. Together.

"Maybe there'll be some kind of clue in the play itself," Hannah suggested.

"Do we all have to read the same copy?" Corey asked. "Can't we get a couple more copies?" He was actually a little nervous about reading something at the same time as Ben and Hannah. He was afraid they'd read a lot faster than him.

"We all need to read Courtney's copy," Ben said.

"She might have written something important in it. And any one of us might catch it."

As it turned out, Ben and Hannah were reading the play so carefully that they didn't read it any faster than Corey did.

Finally, they read the last page. "So Millicent did it," Corey said.

"We already knew that," Ben pointed out.

Hannah sighed. "I was hoping the play might give us some clue, but I didn't pick up on anything."

"It's weird, but the dialogue at the end sounded familiar to me," Ben said. "Like I'd heard it somewhere before."

"We did go to a lot of rehearsals," Hannah remarked.

"Yeah, but we never saw them rehearse the end of the play," Ben countered. He turned to his computer and started typing.

"Wait a minute," Corey said. "Look at this."

He was pointing to the bottom of the last page, where it read: THE END.

"Someone handwrote 'The End,'" he said. "And then the page was photocopied. So Courtney didn't write it. Plus, the handwriting is different from hers."

"You're right," Hannah said, examining the page.

At the same time, Ben had discovered something of his own. "Aha!" Ben said. "Look at this!" He turned his computer monitor, so the other two could see it.

It showed a page full of search results. Ben had typed in a line of dialogue from the end of the play. Every search result mentioned an old movie called *Ghost Mansion*.

"I knew I'd heard that dialogue from somewhere before!" Ben said. "Friday night, when I should have been at the opening night of the play, I was watching a late-night rerun of *Professor When* on the sci-fi channel and I fell asleep. . . ."

"Anyone would fall asleep watching that show," Hannah said, teasing.

"Hey, it's one of my favorites!" Ben protested. "Anyway, when I woke up I saw the last few minutes of this old movie. I didn't catch the title, but it must have been *Ghost Mansion*!"

Hannah suddenly understood. "So you're saying that the guy who wrote *Nobody's Home*"—she looked at the cover of the script—"Theo—"

"Stole his play from an old movie!" Ben announced,

nodding excitedly. "He just changed the title!"

Corey picked up the blackmailer's original note to Courtney and put it beside the last page of the script. "And look!" he said. "The handwriting for 'The End' looks a lot like the handwriting on this note. Which means . . ."

"Theo's the blackmailer!" Ben and Hannah said at the same time.

The next day at school, Ben, Hannah, and Corey crowded into Mrs. Gordon's small office.

Theo sat in a chair, looking miserable.

Mrs. Gordon was looking at the dialogue from *Ghost Mansion* that Ben had printed out for her to see. She also had the original blackmail note and Courtney's copy of the script on her desk. She looked up from the pages, took off her reading glasses, and sighed.

"This is serious, Theo," Mrs. Gordon said. "You plagiarized for a homework assignment, and then you threatened another student to try to keep it secret."

"I'm really sorry," Theo mumbled. "But I never

thought you'd turn my script into the school play. If you performed it, someone was sure to recognize it as an old movie. I had to stop the show."

"How'd you know about Courtney's cheating in gym class?" Ben asked.

Theo shrugged. "We have the same gym teacher, Mr. O'Connor. He left the sixth graders' physical fitness test scores on a chair in the gym. While he was fixing a volleyball net, I was kind of looking at them."

He shot a quick look at Mrs. Gordon, but she was just listening to him, encouraging him to go on. She really was a nice, fair teacher. She made you want to tell the truth.

"I know Courtney from my neighborhood, and she's, you know, small and not very athletic," Theo said. "I thought it'd be funny to see her scores. But when I found them, they were good. Amazingly good. Push-ups, pull-ups—everything. So I looked closer and I could see, like, eraser marks. She'd changed her scores. I couldn't believe Mr. O'Connor hadn't noticed."

"But you didn't tell him?" Hannah asked.

Theo shook his head. "I really wasn't supposed

to be looking at them, you know? And then I remembered Courtney had been chosen as the stage manager for *Nobody's Home*. I was so happy. I had finally figured out a way to stop the play from happening without anyone knowing I had plagiarized it, so I sent her the first note."

He looked at them sincerely. "I wouldn't have told on her. No way. I just wanted to keep the play from going on before I got into trouble."

Mrs. Gordon sighed again. "Well, Theo, I'm afraid you're in trouble now. We're going to have a talk with Principal Inverno."

That Friday night Hannah, Corey, and Ben settled into their seats in the auditorium. It looked as though it was going to be completely full.

"I'm glad they decided to do the play, anyway," Hannah said. "I know Kelly would have been really disappointed after all those rehearsals. And she's really funny in the show."

"But don't they need to have permission from the studio that owns *Ghost Mansion*?" Ben asked.

"They got it," Hannah said. "Kelly said the company that owns the old movie was thrilled that a school was going to perform the script. They're hoping it catches on with other schools. See? It says so right in the program."

Ben found a statement at the front of the program from the company that owned *Ghost Mansion*, wishing the cast lots of good luck with their run of the show. Theo's name was nowhere to be found.

"Hey, that's not all it says in the program!" Corey said. "Look at this!"

He pointed to the back page. At the bottom, in bold print, they read, "The director, cast, and stage manager of the play would like to extend special thanks to Club CSI, without whom this production would not have been possible."

"We're famous!" Corey said, grinning.

David Lewman played the title role in *Oliver!* at the University of Illinois when he was twelve years old. He was also in several school plays and musicals, and even performed in professional shows as an adult. None of them were ever sabotaged. David has written more than sixty-five books starring SpongeBob SquarePants, Jimmy Neutron, the Fairly OddParents, G.I. JOE, the Wild Thornberrys, and other popular characters. He has also written scripts for many acclaimed television shows. David lives in Los Angeles with his wife, Donna, and their dog, Pirkle.